CONNIE BRUMMEL CROOK

Nellie L.

A GEMINI BOOK

First published in 1994 by
Stoddart Publishing Co. Limited
34 Lesmill Road
Toronto, Canada
M3B 2T6
(416) 445-3333

Reprinted March 1995

Canadian Cataloguing in Publication Data

Crook, Connie Brummel
Nellie L.

"Gemini Young Adult."
ISBN 0-7736-7422-5

1. McClung, Nellie L., 1873–1951 — Juvenile literature.
2. Feminists — Canada — Biography — Juvenile literature.
3. Women authors, Canadian (English) — 20th century — Biography — Juvenile literature. I. Title.

HQ1455.N45C76 1994 j305.42′092 C94-931331-9

Cover Design: Brant Cowie/ArtPlus Ltd.
Cover Illustration: David Craig
Typesetting: Tony Gordon Ltd.
Printed in the United States of America

Stoddart Publishing gratefully acknowledges the support of the Canada Council, the Ontario Ministry of Culture, Tourism and Recreation, Ontario Arts Council, and Ontario Publishing Centre in the development of writing and publishing in Canada.

To my aunt,
Pearl Brummel Edmonds,
of Burnaby, B.C.,
who is a constant source of encouragement
in my writing,
and to the memory of my grandmother,
Pearl Salisbury Brummel,
writer of short stories and poems
— to the delight of her grandchildren

Contents

Acknowledgements

I would like to thank Harry Mooney and family along with my sister-in-law Gwen Crook for showing and describing the site of the farm that was homesteaded by the Mooney family. A special thanks to Nellie McClung's grandchildren, especially the Honourable John W. McClung, Jane Brown-John, Marcia McClung, and Nellie McClung, for permission to use quotes from her autobiography, *Clearing in the West.*

Thanks also to the reference department of Trent University Bata Library for helping me find historical background material and Nellie McClung's books, now out of print.

Thanks to Miss Cora Bailey of Peterborough, a teacher for forty years, for answering questions about schools when her mother was teaching; and to Cynthia Rankin, a teacher with the Peterborough County Board of Education for the study guide; and thanks also to

Debbie and Dan Floyd, and Beth Beranger, teachers in Oshawa and Newcastle, for reading and helpful suggestions. A special thanks to Dan for helping me with the football chapter.

A special appreciation goes to my editor, Kathryn Dean, who also saw the potential in Nellie McClung's youth for a young adult story and worked with me toward that end. Thank you for all your questions, helpful suggestions, and detailed editing.

And thanks to Donald G. Bastian, Managing Editor of Stoddart Publishing, and Elsha Leventis for their support and encouragement.

Part One

Prairie Girl

1

"Why can't I race?"

"Because there's no race for the girls, and anyway, it's not proper."

That was like Mother, Nellie thought, scrubbing the kitchen table a little harder. For weeks, Nellie had been looking forward to racing at the Millford picnic, and now, the day before, her mother was making up another rule just to spoil things. That's what she always did when you were starting to have fun. What was the point of doing all this cooking and cleaning if the picnic was going to be boring anyway?

Nellie thought of another angle. "If there isn't a race for the girls, then why can't I run in the boys' race?"

"Nellie L. Mooney, there's no question of your being in any race. Now you just come over here." Mother took Nellie by the arm, led her over to the stool on the opposite side of the kitchen, and sat down in the rocking chair beside it.

"Nellie," she said, her face softening a bit, "you are still young, but there are a few things you must know. Good girls do not run races and they do not show their legs in public."

"But boys show their legs . . . even when they go to church. Why can't girls wear knee pants, too? What's the difference?"

Nellie swung her right leg back and forth beside the stool and twisted a piece of her thick brown bobbed hair around her fingers.

"Now that's enough!" her mother replied. "When you're older, you'll understand. We've been so isolated from others since we came west and I've been so busy, I've failed to train you. But I'll teach you this much: there'll be no racing at this picnic . . . or anywhere else in public for that matter. Now that's final and I don't want to hear any more about it."

Mother got up, and Nellie knew that meant no more pleading. Once her mother had decided something, there was no point in arguing. It was just a waste of breath.

"Don't I wish I could make a dozen juicy pies!" Mother said, smoothing her apron over her brown homespun dress. "There's nothing like a pie, but with no fruit, no eggs, no pumpkins, it's hard. Hannah, get me a jar of molasses from the cellar. And Nellie, you go into the front room and help Lizzie hem dresses. I don't want to hear any more smart talk." It was true what Father said about Mother: she would have no trouble keeping forty people busy.

Hannah got up from the wooden table beside the window where she was peeling potatoes and headed for the back door. Her auburn hair glinted in the June sunlight as she walked across the yard towards the root cellar. Hannah was thirteen, only three years older than Nellie, but Nellie always thought her sister was nearly grown up. After all, she already knew how to read. Nellie didn't. Nellie had been too young to go to school when the Mooneys lived in Ontario. Then, three years ago, in 1880, they had moved to Manitoba, where there was no school yet.

Nellie was not the least bit concerned about this state of affairs, since she planned to be a cowboy when she grew up and cowboys didn't need to learn to read. She knew how to count up to one hundred, and that would be good enough, since she never would have more than a hundred cows. Besides, if she wanted to hear stories, Hannah would always read some to her — in exchange for doing some of her chores.

Nellie opened the door to the front room, where Lizzie was working at the table they had brought with them from their Grey County farmhouse. In her lap, she had what looked like a big pile of white material spotted with yellow and blue dots.

"Here, Nellie, what do you think of this now?" Lizzie held up the dress Nellie was going to wear to the picnic. It had a tight bodice, frilled shoulders called wings that tapered down to the waist, and a full skirt that dropped almost to the ankles.

"It's beautiful, Lizzie. Real, store-boughten material from Ontario. I'm so glad Mother saved it. I'll look just as pretty as Abigail Adams . . ."

Lizzie was Nellie's eldest sister by six years, and she was everybody's friend. She knew how to sew almost anything.

"Here, Nellie, try it on," Lizzie said, holding the dress out to her and brushing back a lock of bright brown hair that had fallen against her forehead. Her skin was so fair that one of the neighbour girls said she washed her face in buttermilk.

Nellie stepped out of her work dress and into the picnic dress and twirled around in front of the horsehair sofa.

"It's so full, Lizzie . . . but it's no good for racing in, is it? Even if Mother did let me race, a skirt like that would just get in my way. And even if I could run in the dress, my drawers would definitely show. Why do drawers always have to be lacy and white?"

"I don't know, Nellie, that's just the way they are. And what difference does the colour make?"

"A big difference. Don't you see? If they were the same colour as my dress, no one would ever notice when my skirt came up."

"Well, I guess you're right! And for you, Nellie L., I think there should be drawers to match all your dresses." She laughed her merry, musical laugh.

"Make me a pair, Lizzie. Please! Just for this one dress. Please, Lizzie, please." Nellie got off her chair and knelt in front of Lizzie with her clasped hands in Lizzie's lap.

"Don't act so silly, Nellie," Lizzie said. "I can't work with you lying on top of the material like that! You know Mother would never let me make you matching drawers. Besides, where would I get the material?"

"There's lots of material right here if you sew the pieces together. And Mother will never need to know. You've saved more material than even she would believe possible." Nellie was whispering now. "Just think . . . I would be the perfect lady and still be able to run around at the picnic. No one would notice if my drawers *did* show."

"I don't know . . . ," Lizzie said in a softer voice, but Nellie knew she was weakening.

"Please make me matching drawers," Nellie whispered one last time.

****

The morning of the picnic, Nellie jumped out of bed and looked out her window. The sun was shining, and all the birds in the world seemed to be singing. Every blade of grain was growing bright green in the fields. Nellie's dog, Nap, was nosing around the barnyard, doing his rounds.

Out past the willows that bordered the creek, she could see orange lilies and wild roses dotting the prairie. Five miles to the northeast was Millford, the little village at the junction of the Souris River and Oak Creek, where the picnic was to be held. To the northwest, the rolling land was spotted with bluffs of poplar, scrub oak, and hawthorne, stretching out to where the rugged greyish blue Brandon Hills loomed on the horizon.

Nellie knew that the land used to be the home of the buffalo. None of the Mooneys had ever seen any of the beasts: the last one had been spotted a year before the family had arrived. But that did not stop Nellie and Hannah from going out onto the prairie, hoping to find one with its great shoulders and shaggy brown fur, feeding on some grassy knoll. They never found any, though, and Nellie would always come home angry at the greedy hunters from the cities who had shot them for no reason. All that remained of the great herds were their bones and buffalo runs, the paths leading to their water holes, where the first faint imprints of the animals' hoofs could just barely be seen.

Nellie wished she had a best friend besides her sister Hannah, but no one lived nearby, so Nap had become her next-best friend. Mr. and Mrs. Burnett, whose farm was two miles south of the Ingrams, the Mooneys' nearest neighbours only a mile to the west, had brought him as a gift that day everyone in the area came to help the Mooneys build their house. He was a tiny ball of black and white fur, part Labrador, and Nellie had spent the whole day carrying him around in a basket. Now he was full grown, but he was still as lively as a puppy.

"Wake up, Nellie!" It was Hannah calling from the bottom of the stairs.

"I *am* awake!" Nellie shouted back as she ran to the washstand. She poured some water in a bowl and scrubbed her face. Then she raced to the other side of the room, took her drawers from under the mattress, where she had hidden them, and began dressing. She caught a glimpse of herself in the little floor mirror tucked under the eaves. Her full drawers, attached to the bodice with four sturdy buttons, looked just like her skirt — at least from across the room. She admired them for a moment, then covered them with her petticoat and matching skirt.

Nellie hurried down the steep stairs to the kitchen. Hannah had already finished her breakfast and was sweeping the floor. Mother was setting jars of pickles and preserves on the wooden table next to the window that looked towards the barn. Lizzie was at one end of the kitchen table, packing pies into a big wicker basket.

Nellie could not believe that her mother had figured out a way to make those pies. There were no eggs, because the weasels had killed their small flock of hens that spring — and you needed eggs to make good pies. But Mother was always resourceful when it came to cooking and mending and fixing things around the house and barn. She must have discovered something to mix with molasses.

Nellie was not so good at doing things like sewing and cooking. But that didn't matter, she thought, as she sat down in front of her bowl of hot porridge. Cowboys just needed to know how to lasso and ride horses. They didn't need to know how to make pies.

"Lizzie, do be careful with those pies. They're not my best creations, but I did find a way to make them without eggs. They're made of butter and molasses and bread crumbs, with vinegar and cinnamon thrown in for flavour. Maybe next year we'll have hens and I can make a proper batch with saskatoon berries."

"Did I hear someone say saskatoon berry pie?" said Father as he stepped in the door with Nellie's brothers, Will and Jack, close behind him.

"No, my dear, molasses pie. The saskatoons will be for next year."

Father hit his balding head with his hand in mock despair, and his brown eyes twinkled. He looked younger today, the way he must have when he was growing up in Ireland. His homespun trousers were pressed sharp, and he was wearing a white shirt and cuff links with horses' heads on them.

Nellie thought her father must be looking forward to the picnic very much. When they had first arrived, three years ago, there was so much work to do and so few neighbours that no one had thought of holding a picnic. Even before then, life had been hard for Father. He'd been driven out of Ireland by the famines in 1830. But he still knew how to have fun. Nellie thought his difficult life should have made him sadder, but he said it was because of all the troubles he'd seen that he knew how important it was to laugh.

Will's eyes were twinkling, too, and he looked more handsome than usual. At twenty-four, he was taller than Father and broad-shouldered but slim. His brown hair curled tightly around his ears, and his cheeks were ruddy from his long hours in the fields.

Then there was Jack, who was fifteen, and just as scruffy-looking as usual. He'd been out to slop the hogs and he looked it, too. "He thinks he knows everything," Nellie thought to herself. Then she said out loud, "You're never going to meet a pretty girl at the picnic looking like that, Jack!"

"And what makes you think I'm interested? I've no time for women, with all the work I have to do around the farm. Besides I don't plan to get married and you know it. When I'm older, I'll live by myself on a quarter-section and keep dogs! They're less trouble than people — especially you."

"Now, Jack and Nellie, that's quite enough," Mother interrupted. "If it weren't picnic day, I'd give you both extra chores this evening."

The prairie was bright and warm as they set out for the picnic at Millford. A gentle wind blew against the grasses and the sweet brier roses. Saskatoon berries were turning red on their branches.

"Look, girls, . . . orange lilies," said Mother, pointing to a clump at the side of the road. "Could you stop, John?" she said, turning to Father. "The girls could pick some for the tables."

Nellie and Hannah jumped down from the wagon and stepped through the coarse, scratchy grass to where the lilies grew. They picked a few of the orange flowers, then ventured a bit farther to pick some roses.

"Hannah," Nellie whispered, turning to her sister when they were out of earshot of the wagon. "I'm thinking about going into the thirteen-and-under race!"

Hannah opened her mouth in disbelief. "How could you possibly do that?"

"I don't know, but I'll figure out a way."

Hannah's blue eyes looked bigger than ever as she stared at Nellie. "I think it would be great if girls could have races, too, but we don't have, and I can't see any way we can change things."

"What do you mean, we can't change things? If you think it would be great, why don't you run in one?"

"Because I'm not a runner, like you, for one thing! But even if I were, why should we fight to do things like that when there are so many other nice things for us to do?"

"*Nice* things! Like what? Like sitting and watching the boys run? It's not fair! Mother is always telling us you were the brightest student in the school, but I'm not so sure about that now."

"What do you mean, Nellie?"

"I mean you might be smart at school, Hannah, but you always just accept things the way they are — and what's so clever about that?"

"I think it's best to do as well as we can with what we have. If everyone did that, we would be much better off."

"Well I *am* doing the best I can . . . I'm a good runner and I'm going to be in that race, Hannah. Somehow, I am."

Hannah and Nellie took their bouquets back to the wagon and climbed onto the bench. Nellie was careful to step on Jack's leg as she went past.

"Ouch! Get away, Nellie. Are you trying to wreck my leg? I'm going in the races, you know."

Mother turned around, and Nellie braced herself for a scolding. But Mother just smiled and said, "What beautiful flowers!" Her usually stern features and firmly set mouth were relaxed today. Nellie fervently wished that more days were picnic days.

"Those flowers will make perfect bouquets for the picnic tables. . . . And another good thing. There will be no whiskey drinking to spoil everyone's fun. . . I've seen too many nice times spoiled with it. Drunken men fighting and swearing in the street, and their women crying and trying to separate them. It was awful sometimes back in Grey County. No fun for anyone, just bad times."

Nellie wasn't really listening to Mother anymore. She was staring straight ahead, thinking about the races.

2

Down by the riverbank women in straw hats were putting food out on tables and men in clean homespun were standing nearby, laughing and telling stories. Nellie started laying out pies on one of the tables loaded with cinnamon rolls and doughnuts, ginger cookies and railroad cake, home-cured ham, chopped lettuce in sour cream and sugar — and now Mother's molasses pies. She was beginning to feel very hungry.

Nellie stepped out of the way as Mrs. Dale from the other side of Millford walked past, wheeling her baby in a sturdy wicker carriage — a special store-bought one her sister had sent from Montreal. She wore a faded brown dress of homespun, but her bonnet had fresh white lace all along the front. Poor Mrs. Dale! She'd been a happy girl like Lizzie just a year ago when she had married, but now she was a thin, tired-looking woman.

At the other end of Nellie's table stood Mrs. Ingram, a stalwart woman with deep blue eyes and long blonde braids that wound around her head. She was talking to her sister, who was visiting from Montreal and dressed in the latest style. She was wearing a new red pleated skirt made of factory cotton — and a matching red straw hat and parasol!

As Nellie stood admiring this outfit, a great clamour broke out behind her. She turned and saw a big democrat pulled by sleek horses with red rosettes on their harness hames. It was packed with young men playing musical instruments.

"Who's that?" Nellie asked Hannah, who had come up beside her.

"Oh, it's the brass band from Brandon. Will told me. Give me a hand unpacking the salad and hams."

"Let's go watch the ball game," Nellie said when they'd finished.

Hannah shook her head. "I'd sooner stay here where it's cooler . . . and Mother wants me to help serve cider."

"Come on, Hannah, it's no fun serving things. And picnics are supposed to be fun!"

"But I like serving. You have the chance to talk to people and do something for them. I don't want to watch some old baseball game. Not right now anyway, when there's work to do. . . But maybe I'll come later."

Nellie raced over to the baseball diamond a few hundred feet away, where the single men were playing against the married ones. She was glad she didn't have to worry about her drawers showing as she ran up near the catcher's box.

Jack was up to bat. Nellie watched breathlessly as he hit a short ball to second. Would he make it to first base? She almost tore off to meet him there, but controlled herself just in time as her father came walking over. He was smiling broadly, and Nellie knew he was wishing he was young enough to be in the game. Jack made it to first. Then a batter sent the ball almost into the bushes a hundred feet beyond the ball diamond, and all the runners made it home.

"I wish I could play," Nellie said with a sigh.

"I wish you could, too," her father said, "but . . . you see there aren't any other young ladies playing. You'd feel a bit lonesome being the only girl."

"No, I wouldn't! Really, I wouldn't, and besides — " Nellie began.

"But how would we know which side to put you on?"

"It doesn't matter. I'd play on either side. And I'd do all right. I can run faster than Jack, and with my polka dot draw — "

"No, Nellie. I'm sorry, but you can't join the game. Your mother wouldn't stand for it." Then she heard him mumble under his breath, "I can't see what harm it'd do . . . but I don't want my daughter talked about even if she is a ten-year-old child." He looked at Nellie's eager brown eyes gazing up at him. "Anyway, it's fun watching, too," he said.

Nellie knew that Father understood. As she watched the ball flying right into the left fielder's hands, she thought again about the races. She started to plan how to do it. She knew there would be a short race and a long race for the thirteens-and-under. It would be hopeless for her to get into the short race, since it would start and end in full sight of everyone. But the long race was a different matter. Not many people would ride half a mile on the cart to get a close-up view of the starting line. The end of the race was the important part, and the finish would come just to the edge of the grounds and a long way from the picnic tables where all the women were gathered.

Nellie wondered who would start the race. If only she could persuade the judge to let her run, she would have a good chance of winning even if she was shorter than most children her age. Didn't she and Nap run over the fields all the way back to the pasture every night? And that was two miles. But she always carried her skirt and petticoat, since no one could see her there.

More people were coming now to see who was winning the ball game. There were even a few women watching. Her father squinted proudly at the growing crowd. "There are farmers here from as far north as Brandon and as far south as the Tiger Hills," he said.

When the married men won the ball game, Father and Nellie cheered, though they were disappointed that Jack's side had lost. Jack walked over to them, looking dejected.

"Oh, well, Jack, don't worry. If you learn how to hit the ball with the bat, maybe you'll have better luck next time!" Nellie said before she could stop herself.

"Good job, Jack," Father said. Then he turned to Nellie. "And Nellie, is that any way to talk to your brother?"

"Well . . . he — "

"Well, nothing. Now I'm heading over to talk to some of the old geezers at the tables, so Jack, you take care of Nellie till dinnertime."

Jack grimaced and rolled his eyes at Bert Ingram, who had just walked up beside him. Bert was Hannah's age, and to Nellie, he seemed a real man of the world.

"You sure know how to spoil things," Jack grumbled when Father was out of earshot. "I don't want you near the long races."

"Oh, come on, Jack," Bert said. "She can't do any harm. She's not going to be in our way. She'll just watch."

Jack looked away from Bert and grimaced at Nellie. "Why don't you go in the race if you're so smart? The ladies won't miss you, that's for sure. You're not too swift when it comes to setting tables and all that women's stuff."

"You're just jealous because I'm faster than you. And I'm coming with you whether you like it or not."

A wagon drew up to the ball diamond to pick up the runners and take them to the starting line. "Come on, Bert," Jack shouted as he ran towards it. "Let's get away from this pest." Jack and Bert swung over the edge and into the wagon box, but Nellie was close behind. She scrambled up and sat on a bench along the side. "Oh, Jack," she said, "I have a new song for you." She sang:

> The rocky Jack Thomas
> The hedger and ditcher,
> Although he was poor
> Never cared to be richer.

"Get out of this wagon right now," Jack yelled. "You know I hate that song. And women aren't allowed in here anyway. Right, Bert? Right. So get out before I throw you out. No women, do you hear me?"

"Hello, everyone," said a distinctly female voice, belonging to Mrs. Ingram, who was climbing into the wagon and actually managing to do it in a ladylike way. "I don't suppose you have room for one more lady. I see little Nellie's already here, so I thought I'd join you. I want to see that Bobbie gets into the long race."

"Bobbie," Nellie thought, "*little* Bobbie." She rolled her eyes up to the sky.

Jack shifted grumpily out of Mrs. Ingram's way.

Nellie didn't know whether she was more relieved or upset because of Mrs. Ingram. On the one hand, her arrival meant that Jack could not kick Nellie out of the wagon. On the other, it meant that Nellie was going to be stuck riding in the wagon with Bert Ingram's horrible younger brother, Bob.

Just a month ago Mrs. Ingram had come over with Bob for a visit — and to show off Bob's reading skills. He was half a year younger than Nellie, but he was already reading things like Aesop's *Fables*. That afternoon he had stood up in his proper tweed Sunday suit and read out one fable after the other in his loud, squeaky voice.

Nellie had figured out a way to get back at him. When they went out to play, she'd told him about a shortcut through the barnyard, and he'd been foolish enough to take it. Of course, he'd come out the other end covered with mud and pig manure. It's true he'd winked at Nellie when his mother started scolding him for ruining his good suit, so maybe he had a little spunk after all. But he was still a show-off, the way he read to adults all the time — just to impress them.

Nellie looked around and saw Bob trying to swing his leg over the side. But he was too short, so he had to step on the stump of wood placed at the back of the wagon for the ladies to get in. His face was red, and he slumped down beside Mrs. Ingram.

Well, Nellie thought, she and Bob would be in the same race, and one thing was sure — she wouldn't have to worry about Bob beating her.

"Hey, little boy, this is the thirteen-and-under and the fifteen-and-under, not the five-and-under," Jack yelled. "You must be in the wrong race." Bob slouched down another notch.

"Any room for me?" a familiar voice called out. Hannah stepped onto the stump of wood and into the wagon. Nellie squeezed over and motioned Hannah to her side.

The wagon started to move ahead.

"Are you still going to do it?" Hannah whispered to Nellie.

Nellie nodded.

Bert was the only boy who might be a challenge in the thirteen-and-under, and then there was Jack in the fifteen-and-under.

"I've been racing all summer," Bert said in a loud voice. "I wouldn't be surprised if I got to the fifteen-and-under."

"Maybe, but then I'll give you a run for your money, Bert Ingram."

Bert smiled back at Jack. "Well, we'll see about that."

The wagon stopped abruptly, and the boys all pushed out ahead of the girls and Mrs. Ingram. Nellie knew they'd want to get the best possible starting positions. The starting line was about a hundred feet from the wagon and stretched over to the trees at the far side of the clearing.

"We'll wait fifteen minutes for runners in the short race who'll be entering the long race," bellowed Mr. Burnett, the race organizer. He was a big, jovial man, whose arms and face were a deep red from being out in the sun and the wind all the time.

Nellie walked over to him. "Mr. . . . Mr. Burnett, I want to ask you something."

"You're having a good time, are you, young lady?" he said cheerfully, not really paying attention because he was trying to make everyone happy.

"Oh, yes, Mr. Burnett, but . . ." Nellie hesitated.

"What's the problem?"

Nellie tried to keep her voice casual so Mr. Burnett would not see how anxious she was. "I want to run in this race. I know it's just for boys, but why not? I race with my brothers all the time."

Mr. Burnett looked at Nellie with surprise, and he laughed. "Well, yes. Why not?" Nellie heard him mumble. Then he said, "I'm afraid your father wouldn't like it, Nellie."

"Well, he lets me race with my brothers all the time, and besides, he'll probably never know because with all the boys in the race, I'll probably drop out before we reach the picnic grounds. People will think I'm just one of the spectators like Mrs. Ingram. You could even pick me up in the wagon."

Mr. Burnett laughed again. "Well . . . so you want to know the thrill of the race . . . starting off at the signal. I remember it myself. I was a runner in my day." He smiled and then winked. "Now, you go to the far side of the starting line." Nellie knew he was hoping she wouldn't be noticed too much over near the trees and away from where the few spectators were standing. But she didn't care. She was in the race!

Nellie darted around the boys taking up their positions and over to the far side of the starting line. Hannah followed her and stood only a few feet away. She was smiling a little.

"What are you doing here?" shouted Billy Day, one of the neighbour boys who would be going to the new school the local men were building. He left his position and came over to Nellie and looked her straight in the eye as he waited for an answer.

Nellie smiled smugly. "What does it look like I'm doing?"

Four more boys sauntered over. "What's a *girl* doing in the boys' race?" Billy said, now that he had a proper audience. "And you're a shrimp to boot!" More boys pushed into a tight circle around her. Then the rest of them left their positions to see what was causing the excitement.

"Afraid of the competition, boys?" Nellie asked, putting her chin in the air.

"Leave her alone," someone said in a timid voice. Nellie looked around and was surprised to see that it was Bob.

The boys all laughed, and one put on a high-pitched voice and said, "Don't you touch my little friend, or I'll . . ." He bent over laughing at his own cleverness.

"Take up your positions for the thirteen-and-under race," Mr. Burnett shouted. He had walked over to Nellie's end of the starting line. The boys scuffled back to the line and elbowed each other for their original spots.

Nellie pulled her skirt and petticoat up enough to rest her hand on her leg, and balanced to go. She felt more determined than ever now. She must win this race. She must.

"Hurrah for Nellie!" Hannah shouted. Her high-pitched voice carried to the far line of spectators.

"What's Nellie doing there?" said someone who sounded like Mrs. Ingram.

"On your mark . . ." Mr. Burnett bellowed, "get set . . . Go!"

3

With fast, light steps, Nellie shot ahead of the others. She could hear the steady pounding of feet on the ground behind her.

So far, she was keeping her lead, but . . . for how long? Already she could feel her skirt and petticoat pulling on her legs.

The boys were probably pacing themselves and would soon come sailing by . . . and this bloomin' skirt . . .

The thumping sounds were getting louder . . .

Billy Day went by her almost silently. "He *is* fast," she thought.

Another boy passed . . . and another . . . and then three boys almost neck and neck. Nellie knew she was twice as fast as this in the pasture when she carried her dress and ran in her drawers. If only . . .

Then Bob went labouring by. That did it!

She loosened the buttons on her skirt and petticoat and jumped out of them. She was free now, free as the wind, and she ran as if she were going for the cows. Breathing easily, she flew over the pathway unhampered. She had a lot of lost ground to make up . . .

She passed Bob first. She could hear him panting. Then she went by a clump of boys; their feet were pounding the ground almost in unison as she sped by them.

Finally she looked up and saw just one more ahead — Billy Day!

She would beat him, too. She must! The distance was shortening between them. She could hear his breathing now, and saw that his baggy shirt was wet with perspiration.

As she spurted ahead with a sudden burst of energy, so did Billy. He was holding his lead. Then he turned around and their eyes met. She saw surprise and even a glint of fear.

In those few seconds, Nellie moved up beside him and kept pace with him even though she took two strides to his one.

He was breathing heavily now. She pretended he was Nap, and they were racing in the fields . . .

Nellie did not see the two men holding the rope across the road, who were waiting with keen eyes to judge who was the winner. She did not see the others nearby who were there to mark the second- and third-place winners. Nor did she see the crowd of men and women who had gathered to cheer the victors. She saw only the rope across the finish line and she ran for it as she had never run before.

With a sudden spurt, she sped ahead and crossed over the rope that the men had stretched across the ground as the runners approached.

She had won!

She waited for the applause. But no cheer came — only a deadly silence. She slowed to a stop a few feet beyond the line and turned quickly to see Billy Day crossing over the rope with two other boys close behind.

Now she could hear loud cheers and was surprised to see that a huge crowd had gathered at the finish line.

The judge grabbed Billy by the shoulder and shouted, "The winner is Billy Day."

"Billy Day?" Nellie opened her mouth in disbelief. "The winner is *not* Billy Day!" But she had no time to protest further. Her father had rushed over to her and was wrapping his brown knitted coat around her legs. Then Nellie suddenly remembered her petticoat and skirt. She had thought no one would notice.

"Nellie, you are quite some runner," Father said, trying to sound severe, "but this was not the right way to go about it . . ."

Just then Hannah came running up with the lost petticoat and skirt. Nellie was just buttoning the waistband when Mother arrived. Someone must have told her what happened.

"Come with me, young lady," Mother said sternly. "I'll tend to you when we get home. In the meantime, you'll not be out of my sight."

Red-faced and defeated, Nellie marched dutifully behind her mother. She had won that race. She had. How could they say Billy was the winner when he wasn't! They hadn't even mentioned her. They hadn't said her run was disqualified because girls weren't allowed in the race. Instead they had treated her as if she didn't exist. It wasn't fair.

She knew her mother wouldn't understand. As they reached the picnic tables under the shade of the poplar trees, a group of ladies who had been staring at Nellie turned away. "Put out some plates along this side." Mother said. "We'll be serving these two tables."

The ladies had finished setting out the food and had decided to share their dishes over several tables. "I do love to have a taste of someone else's food," Mother often said, even though Nellie knew her pies were probably the best. But Nellie didn't feel hungry anymore.

"Don't worry, Nellie," Hannah said just behind her. "You ran a fine race!"

"What do you mean, 'Don't worry,'" Nellie hissed. "I should have won the prize. I was the winner. How could the judges just ignore me?"

"Well, sometimes it's best just to accept things as they are. But, Nellie, I wish that . . . "

Mother turned and stared at Hannah, who suddenly found something she had to get out of one of the food baskets.

Before long, the men started coming towards the tables. All the women smiled and stood back while the men pushed into their places. Reverend Thomas Hall, the minister from the new Methodist church, gave thanks to God for the meal, but Nellie did not really hear the prayer.

The men and boys over ten were eating now. The women, as well as their little children, would eat later because they were too busy pouring tea and coffee. Nellie was serving the apple cider and had to walk past the fire where the teakettles were boiling and Mother and Mrs. Ingram were working and talking. She could imagine that Nellie L. Mooney was the subject of the conversation, so she stood still, trying to listen.

"Don't you stand there with your mouth agape, Nellie," said Mother, who had a great talent for watching her daughter even when she was deep in conversation.

"There's a lot of thirsty men to be served and they'll be parchin' if you don't get a move on."

As Nellie poured the cider, she wondered why her mother was so angry. She should be proud that her daughter had won that race. And unless people looked closely, they never would have noticed that she had run in drawers rather than a full skirt. After all, it was only when she took long strides that anyone could tell the difference. "I just don't understand why mother is so mean," thought Nellie as she slopped some cider into Mr. Burnett's cup.

"Oh, sorry, Mr. Burnett, I wasn't watching what I was doing."

"Oh, that's all right, Nellie Mooney," Mr. Burnett said quietly. "You can't be good at everything, and if I were you, I'd be happy I was such a fast runner!"

Her brother Will was sitting across from Mr. Burnett. He looked up at Nellie and gave her his gentle smile.

Nellie couldn't believe her eyes or her ears, but she smiled at Will and the big, red-faced man, and walked away with a lighter heart.

Now she had to go over to the table where the boys were eating. A few of them glanced up and nudged each other when they saw her coming. She poured cider into all their cups, but when she got to Billy Day, he wouldn't even look at her.

After the meal was over and the men had gone for the pony races, the women cleared away all the dishes. They would miss the ponies, but they might just make it in time to see the slow-ox race.

Nellie would have given just about anything to see the pony races. Surely Mother would let her go. There was no danger of her running in that one! But the answer was no. "You are going to stay in my sight for the entire afternoon," Mother said. "I want you handy to help when I need you."

Mrs. Dale, the tired young mother with the faded brown dress, smiled shyly at Nellie. She was holding her new baby in her arms and sitting on one of the benches. "I wish I had a strong young lady like your Nellie to help me with Geordie," she said to Mother. "I'd get her to push the carriage for a while. Maybe Geordie would drop off to sleep."

"Nellie wouldn't mind, I'm sure," Mother said, giving Nellie a look that meant she had no choice in the matter.

"I'd love to," Nellie said. Since she was the youngest, she had never cared for a baby at home. She thought it might be fun for a little while. At least that way she could get out of cleaning up the tables.

The young mother fixed the baby's blankets tightly around him. "You can wheel him over by those trees," she said, pointing to a grove of poplars. "That's a good distance from the races, but it's close enough for you to watch. If Geordie fusses too much, just bring him back. Don't try to take him out of the carriage." Nellie was starting to like Mrs. Dale, and felt certain she was in her own way trying to reward her for winning the race.

Nellie gleefully grabbed the carriage. "As long as you keep pushing him, he'll love it," Mrs. Dale added. That was no problem for Nellie. She happily bumped the carriage along the grass and headed for the poplar grove.

Geordie was sleeping quietly now, and Nellie had not too bad a view of the pony races from where she sat. Sunlight and dust shimmered over the racetrack, and Nellie could hear the men's muffled shouts. Mr. Dale's Shetland pony won, and a garland of orange lilies was hung around his neck.

Mr. Dale had had a busy day. He had played baseball on the winning team, combed his pony, and overfed his ox. Now, mopping his brow, he led his pony away. But soon he returned, flopped down on the grass in the shade of a few Manitoba maples near the track, and began to chat with a group of men resting there after their big noon meal.

Then the Brandon band, which was seated at one end of the track, began to play "Rule Britannia" and "The Maple Leaf." The ground shook, and the music seemed to come from everywhere at once. Nellie was content again, knowing that Father and Will, as well as Mr. Burnett and Mrs. Dale, appreciated her race. Mother and all those other ladies were the only ones who did not understand.

"Nellie, Nellie, look what Mr. Burnett has for us!"

"Oh, no, it's Bob Ingram," Nellie thought. He and Mr. Burnett were walking towards her.

"Look, a whole pail full of chocolates and oranges and bananas," Bob said.

"Bananas? What's that?"

"You can have one of each, Nellie." Mr. Burnett smiled, showing her what he had taken from the barrel. "Oranges and bananas straight from the tree — via Rapid City and Brandon — and chocolates from Toronto."

Nellie ate the orange and put the chocolate in her pocket to save it for when she would really need it — after Mother had punished her. Then she bit into the banana.

"It tastes just like flannel, Mr. Burnett," she said, making a face.

"I don't like mine either. What's so special about them?" Bob complained.

"Well, I guess they're an acquired taste — but they

are a delicacy. I think the Queen eats them," Mr. Burnett said with a big smile.

As Mr. Burnett and Bob Ingram moved on, Nellie put her hand in her pocket to check how the chocolate was doing. To her horror, it was melting and oozed out between her fingers. There was no point in keeping it now, so she ate it, licking her fingers so hard the skin almost came off.

Nellie wiped her moist hands on her dress and looked towards the racetrack again. She could see Will leading their Jed to where a lot of other oxen were standing. The slow-ox race was about to begin. This was a backwards race. The winner was the one who came in last. Neighbours would ride each other's oxen, trying to get them to speed to the finish line. One person would slap the animal from behind and someone else would coax it from the front with a pan of oats. Nellie was glad that none of the oxen would be beaten and hurt, since whips and switches were not allowed.

It looked as if Jed would be ridden by Jimmy Sloan, who worked for Mr. Burnett. The four oxen were led to the starting line, and three of them trotted off as the crowd began to cheer. But gentle Jed just ambled along, shaking his ears and ignoring Jimmy, who was waving his straw hat at him and yipping like a coyote.

For a few minutes it looked as if Jed was going to win. But suddenly he sped forward, galloping like a wild horse and bouncing his rider up and down. The crowd fell silent and Nellie's heart raced. Jed threw Jimmy to the ground. Then, his massive side streaming red with blood, he turned and started heading straight towards her and the baby. His head was lowered, and he was bellowing in pain.

Someone screamed, and the baby began to cry. Nellie

grabbed Geordie from the carriage and started to run. But it was too late.

Then, glancing back at Jed, Nellie froze in terror as the ox charged.

At the last minute, Jed turned and crashed into the bushes beside the poplars.

Nellie's knees went funny and she could not walk. Someone came over and grabbed the baby out of her arms. The next thing Nellie knew, Mother was in front of her, holding out her arms. Nellie fell into them. Then she felt herself being lifted into the wagon and onto the buffalo robe.

Indignant and grumbling voices drifted through the soft cloud-like silence enfolding Nellie. Then she heard things being loaded onto the wagon.

Soon the wagon began to move. Someone sat close beside her and said, "Wake up, Nellie. We're headed home now." It was Lizzie.

"It isn't bedtime yet," Hannah was saying. "Wake up, Nellie. You're all right."

"I know. I'm fine," Nellie repeated, but then she would fall asleep again. Between times, she caught bits of the conversation.

"It was the damned spurs!" Father said. "Jimmy Sloan used his spurs!"

Mother spoke out loudly, "It wasn't the spurs, John. It was the liquor! That brass band from Brandon brought in whiskey. Jimmy is one of the best boys in the country and never would have used his spurs if he hadn't been drunk. It was the liquor, John."

"I know, I know." Father sighed. "I'll miss Jed, I will. He was a good worker and such a gentle beast. Now he'll be useless as a dray ox. I'll have to fatten him this summer and send him to market in the fall."

"We have good neighbours, though, John," Nellie

heard Mother saying. "What a blessing! It did my heart good to see Frank Burnett and Mr. Dale bite into my molasses pie. Next year I'll make some lemon pies that will melt in their mouths!"

"Not a bad day, all in all," Nellie thought, snuggling down into the itchy buffalo robe. But then she remembered about her skirt and petticoat and wondered what sort of punishment Mother was storing up for her. "Oh, well," she thought. "I'll worry about that tomorrow."

4

It was another bright day, and Nellie was inside the henhouse, feeding Nancy, their new hen. In the two weeks since the community picnic, Nellie had not been running around the farm, as usual. Mother had kept her busy scrubbing all the floors in the house. But now that her punishment was over, Nellie was free to roam about once more. She was even happy to feed the hens. A week before, Mrs. Burnett, Mrs. Ingram, and two other neighbour women had arrived in a wagon, each carrying a box with a hen in it. Mother's eggless molasses pie had become famous, and so had the story about the Mooneys having no hens. So their neighbours had come to their rescue by donating some healthy birds.

Nellie and Hannah wanted to name the hens Nancy, Mary, Georgina, and Annie, after the women who had brought them, but Mother did not like the idea. The names of respectable married women, she said, were not to be spoken in the barnyard. Nellie and her brothers and sisters still used the names, though — but not in front of Mother.

Nancy had been one of Mrs. Ingram's favourite hens in spite of her stubborn character. One winter she had spent an entire night roving outside the Ingrams' henhouse and was found the next morning leaning against the henhouse wall with her feathers fluffed out and her temper ruffled. They took her into the house and fed her bran mash, but the ends of her claws were frozen so badly she could no longer scratch for food.

The next spring, in spite of her frozen toes, she had hatched six eggs. Of course, she could not scratch for seeds to feed her chicks, so she walked straight up to Mrs. Ingram's kitchen and cackled out that she wanted them to be fed. From then on, the Ingrams took bread soaked in milk out to Nancy and her brood every day. Now the Mooneys were doing the same.

All the hens lived in a little log henhouse that had a wooden floor, one window, and a door that had to be closed each night to prevent mink or weasels from getting in. It was Nellie's job to make sure the henhouse door was closed.

As Nellie put Nancy's food in front of her, she thought how strange it was that Mother could be so kind to this new hen and so stern with her children.

Just as Nellie stepped out into the sunlight, her father came hurrying in from the laneway with a scythe in his hand. He sat down with a hard thump on the little bench outside the henhouse and began to sharpen the scythe.

"How come you're back so early, Father?"

"I forgot to take the sharpening stone along with me this morning. But I'm glad for a break. And how's my Nellie L. this morning?"

"Fine." Nellie always liked the musical sound of "Nellie L." the way her father said it. The "L." stood for her middle name, Letitia. "Mother is letting me out more now. I was so sick of scrubbing floors. At last, they're done."

Father gave Nellie his kind smile. "Sit a bit," he said. Nellie sat down on the bench beside him as he continued to sharpen the blunt end of the scythe.

"Why is Mother so strict?" Nellie asked.

"Well, that's a good question, Nellie L. She is a serious woman. I think it's because she's Scotch. They're a bit stern, but the greatest people in the world for courage and backbone. The Irish are different; not so steadfast or reliable, but very pleasant. Irish people have had so much trouble, they've had to sing and dance and laugh and fight to keep their hearts from breaking."

"I'm glad you are Irish," Nellie said, smiling at Father.

"Well, you don't want to have a world full of Irish people either, Nellie L. Just think, if everyone sang and danced, no one would get any work done. You know, when Christ was on earth, he showed us that we can be polite and pleasant, and full of fun and fond of music, and yet serious, too, and earnest. We should all try to combine these things."

"Well, Mother should be more playful then."

"That may be so, but then it would mean the Irish types, like you and me, would have to do more work!"

"I guess so," Nellie sighed, "but not now. Sing me the song about the red petticoat again."

Father went on sharpening his scythe and sang:

Shule, shule, shule, agra
It's time can only aise my woe
Since the lad o' me heart
From me did part

Shedate, avoureem, schlana
I'll dye me petticoat,
I'll dye it red
And through the world
I'll beg me bread,
I wish in me heart
That I was dead.
Schedate, avoureen, schlana.

Nellie gazed up at her father and smiled. The words of the song were sad, but the two of them were happy just the same.

****

Nellie awoke with a start. In the still silence of the summer night, she could hear Hannah breathing gently beside her, and Lizzie across the room. What had awakened her? She tried not to breathe and listened for sounds in the darkness. The willows were rustling beside the creek, but there was something else, too. It sounded like hens cackling. Nellie tightened her lips as she realized what had happened. She had forgotten to shut the henhouse door. All that talk about wanting to dance and play this afternoon and look where she was now. She had just proved once more that she was totally irresponsible.

She jumped out of bed in the pitch darkness, grabbed her boots, and tiptoed to the door. As she walked down the creaking stairs, one step at a time, her heart thumped with fear. What if the weasels and mink had invaded? That very spring the weasels had tunnelled up through the dirt floor of their henhouse and left the birds lying dead on the floor with punctured throats. Now their henhouse had a wooden floor as weasel-protection, but that wouldn't do any good if the door was wide open. What weasel would not leap at the opportunity of a hen massacre?

Nellie closed the back door silently. No sound came from the henhouse. If the weasels had been there, they had done their dirty work and gone. Nellie stepped cautiously through the open doorway and tripped over a soft furry object.

"Nap!" she shouted with joy. "Nap, dear Nap." The dog was in the doorway, and Nellie knew in that minute that her hens would be safe. For Nap had lain there to guard them. With great relief, she felt her way around the henhouse. Nancy and all the hens were fine. She breathed a sigh of relief, walked out, and shut the door. As she turned to hurry back to the house, she realized for the first time how dark it was outside.

A hand grabbed her arm, but before she could scream, another hand clapped across her mouth. "Keep quiet unless you want Father out here," Jack said. "I know what you've done and that's enough. No point waking Father and telling him."

"Well, you don't need to scare me half to death. And what are *you* doing out here anyway?"

"I just want you to know that I saw everything. If it weren't for Nap, we'd be without any hens again."

"Well, it's none of your business. Don't you have anything better to do? Goodnight!" Nellie ran for the house with Jack close behind.

****

The next morning Jack told everyone at the breakfast table that Nellie had forgotten to close the henhouse door. Nellie could think of nothing else all day. As she did her house and barn chores, she planned her revenge. She was determined to get even.

Late in the afternoon, Nellie ran into the kitchen and shouted, "Jack, Jack, your horse Kate must have broken out of the barnyard. I saw her wade through the creek and head towards Millford. You'd better hurry." Jack almost choked on the leftover molasses pie he was eating. Then he jumped up from the table and rushed out the door. Nellie bent over with laughter as she watched him run down the slope to the barn to saddle up Billy.

Jack's big piece of pie still sat on the table along with the empty pie tin. Nellie could see it was the last piece, so with another chuckle, she gobbled it down.

Nellie had just finished licking her fork when Jack came back in with a roar. "Kate's in the barn," he bellowed, opening his eyes wide. "Father or Will must have put her in. What made you think she'd run away?" Nellie smiled and rolled her eyes. Telltale marks of molasses still lingered around her mouth.

"Nellie, you'll pay for this!" Jack dived across the room. Nellie dodged and grabbed a ball of yarn from the table. She threw it straight at him, but Jack got out of the way and the ball went into the front room and hit mother's special blue vase on top of the whatnot. The vase teetered and fell to the floor with a crash.

Just then Mother stepped into the kitchen. "What was that noise?"

Jack and Nellie looked at the floor.

"Did something break?"

"Well . . . I think it was . . . your blue vase," Nellie mumbled.

Mother walked into the front room and stared in disbelief at her favourite vase, now in pieces on the floor.

"Who did this?" she said in a deadly calm voice.

Jack looked at Nellie. Finally Nellie mumbled, "I did, but it's all Jack's fault."

"I don't know why she thinks it's my fault unless maybe she didn't think I'd dodge when she flung that ball at me," grumbled Jack.

Mother looked from one to the other. "Jack," she said. "Go out and do your barn chores. I'll talk to you later." When Jack was gone, she turned to Nellie. "Now you, young lady, are going to go right up to your bedroom and stay there until tomorrow morning . . . and without supper, I might add."

"What about Jack? Will he have to go without supper?"

"Jack has to eat to work on the farm. He can't miss a meal. The farm work is important. Now march up those stairs."

****

Nellie watched the shadows deepening after the sun had set. Supper was long past. No one had come up to see her. She knew Lizzie would have sneaked upstairs with a bite for her if she could have, but there were times when even Lizzie could not escape Mother's all-seeing eyes.

Just when she had given up hope, she heard her father's slow footsteps coming up the stairs. His and Mother's big bedroom was downstairs, so he must be coming to see her.

"How's my Nellie L.?" he said, smiling as he came through the door.

"It's not fair," Nellie muttered gloomily. "Jack should have missed his supper, too."

"Well, that's life. It's not always fair. And we just have to learn to accept things the way they are," said Father with a sigh. He sat down on the bed beside Nellie. "You must learn to be more careful, Nellie L. Your mother brought that vase all the way from the old country. It was her mother's."

"I'm sorry. I didn't mean to break her vase. It was an accident."

"I know that and she knows that. Still it's broken. She and Lizzie are trying to paste it together, but it's pretty badly smashed."

"I am very sorry," Nellie mumbled, looking down.

"Let's not talk about it anymore now. There's no point in crying over spilled milk for too long."

"Well, Jack has got to stop poking his nose into my business. I hate him, Father. I swear I do." Nellie hadn't intended to say that. The words had just slipped out. She looked up at her father's surprised face, but he said nothing. Instead he pulled a hand from behind his back and offered Nellie three of Mother's big oatmeal cookies. Nellie grabbed them and started munching away. "I shouldn't have said that about Jack. You won't tell him, will you, Father?"

"I won't tell him," he said in a kind voice. "I'm good at forgettin'."

5

"Don't go so fast, Nellie! You're tearing the basket out of my hand." Hannah and Nellie were carrying ham sandwiches and cold well water to the men who were helping Father with the harvest. They were in the west field, half a mile from the house, so there was a long way to go. Nellie was pulling on the basket handle, trying to get Hannah to walk faster. She knew the men had started work at six in the morning and would be hungry by now. It was past nine o'clock.

They ran past the barn, with Nap pelting along beside them, barking and nipping at clumps of grass along the way. The ripening grain made golden squares and bands on the prairie, and blue haze shrouded the horizon. It was early September, and the whole community was alive with the sounds of harvest.

"I hope the binder is holding up," Hannah said,

panting. "Because if not, Father will be very, very upset."

Nellie nodded knowingly. In late June a salesman had come to their area from Toronto and sold binders to almost all the farmers. They looked marvellous, but now they all kept breaking down. Nearly every night, Father, Will, or Jack had to go all the way to Brandon to get new parts.

Now, to make matters worse, Mr. Mackenzie was scheduled to arrive with his threshing machine at noon. If the binder broke down, the grain would not be ready for threshing, and that would be a problem. Mr. Mackenzie was finishing at the Ingrams this morning and the Mooneys' crops were the only ones left in the neighbourhood.

Once he moved his machine out of the area, Mr. Mackenzie would not be back for some time. Then the Mooneys would risk losing part of the overripe crop from this last field in a wind or rain storm. This grain was too ripe now to handle much, and so they would not want to stack it at the barn as they had their earlier crops.

When the neighbouring famers had completed the threshing next door, they had left Mr. Mackenzie oiling his machine in the Ingram's backyard and come over to help the Mooneys finish up their work.

Hannah and Nellie breathed a sigh of relief as they entered the field. The binder was working. They could see Will sitting high on the seat. The machine was humming along nicely, but there was a break in the lever that held the sheaves until a number could be dumped on the ground together. So Father and Jack were following close behind, gathering into windrows the sheaves that had tumbled out ahead of time. George Ingram and Nathan Smith had already arrived with their teams and were headed for the windrows. Frank Burnett and Samuel Dale had started to fork the freshly cut sheaves onto the wagons. The other half of the field that Jack and Will had stooked yesterday into upright bunches of eight sheaves each would be left until these were loaded.

One by one, the men noticed Hannah and Nellie standing in the sun with the food basket and the water pail. They stuck their forks in the ground and strode towards the edge of the field.

"Well, you finally got here!" Jack yelled from part way across the field. "We're working like slaves, all parched and starving, and you just take your time!"

Jack strode up to Nellie first, grabbed the dipper, and scooped into the pail. Sweat was dripping off his nose and chin. He took a long drink of the cold, fresh well water before the others even fell in line. Will was the only one who didn't come in for a snack, since he was running the binder. They could not afford to lose a minute with that machine.

"Jack is always such a grouch," Nellie grumbled to Hannah.

"He's been working hard," Hannah said calmly.

"He's been working hard? How about *us?"*

"Well, women's work is different," Hannah said, pulling the white linen cloth off the top of the wicker basket and letting the men help themselves to the hot buttered biscuits and ham and mustard sandwiches. She set the basket on the ground and walked a few feet away.

"But, Hannah, women's work is just as difficult."

"Yes, in its way, I guess."

Nellie sat down beside Hannah and listened to what the men had to say.

"Thanks for the extra help, men," Father said as they

all stood eating. "I sure do appreciate it, and when the thresher gets here, I hope we can keep ahead of that thirsty machine. The boys and I won't have the field all cut until dark, but still I'd hate to leave it and only thresh the wheat we've already stacked by the barn. This wheat's already overripe." The men knew the stack would keep fine till they could get to it. But the overripe wheat in the field would shell on the ground and be wasted if it were not soon harvested.

"We're glad to give you a hand," said Frank Burnett. "We never know when we might be in the same fix ourselves, with our binder not working proper. And it's comforting to know we got good neighbours willing to help. You'd do the same for any one of us."

Father smiled back at Frank and picked off a head of wheat. "Sure, and it is a grand country that can grow forty bushels of this to the acre," he said. "It's great to be alive on a day like this, with enough to eat and a bed to lie on."

"That's as may be," said Nathan Smith with a deep frown, "but life ain't always easy out here." His deep-set eyes and bushy eyebrows looked darker than usual. Nellie leaned forward a bit to hear what he was going to say.

Everyone nodded sympathetically. Nathan Smith had just lost his wife. He brushed back a tear with the back of his dust-covered hand.

"Poor Sarah was still in her prime when she just up and died, and me with all the fall work upon me. It wasn't like her to just quit."

"No, that's true. But I guess there's one good thing," George Ingram said. "She wasn't sick for long."

"No, she wasn't. She never cost me a doctor's bill."

"Sarah was a good woman," Father said.

"That she was, that she was. She was as strong as any

horse I have on the place. And often when I'd be up in bed, I'd hear her downstairs poundin' out loaves of bread. When I got up in the mornin', she'd have it all baked, waitin' for me. She was a great wife!"

Nellie stared at the wheat stubble on the ground, wondering when Mrs. Smith had had the time to sleep. She knew many farmers' wives died young, and she started to feel angry at the farmers who treated their wives like plough horses.

"Well, you'll be busy now cooking for the lot of you," Father went on. "Is it six or seven children you have?"

"Six. And the oldest one only nine, but she's trying. I left her minding the others today. I can't help feeling that Sarah let me down, going so sudden like. I don't mind saying she's sure left me in some mess."

Some of the men nodded while others looked away. "Lettie will go over from time to time to give you a hand," Father said. "I'm sure the other farm women will, too."

"It's true there's nothing like a good woman to do the work of a horse," Samuel Dale said, wiping his mouth with the back of his hand. "That is, unless the schools get their way and start teaching all the females to read. I never went to school and I done all right. I don't want my kids to get the feeling they know more than I do."

"Can't say I agree with you there, Dale," Father said. "The more kids know, the better. We can't live in ignorance and still progress."

"You're just like the women, Mooney. They're all for learnin', but I want my kids to stay and help on the farm. And if they don't know any better, they'll stay. Ignorance holds families together!"

Nellie thought of Mrs. Dale and what a life she was going to have with this man. She was about to say as much to Hannah, but she was interrupted by the sudden silence as the cranky binder stopped humming. Will, who was normally even-tempered, let out a loud curse and stomped around it. Everyone rushed over to see what was the matter.

The tongue that hitched the binder to the horses had snapped, and there was a big crack in the wood, which had obviously been smoothed down and painted over. Will stomped around some more and looked at the crack without saying anything. When Father took a closer look at the tongue, he started ranting in Irish, stopping every so often to pat Will on the shoulder and say, "Take it aisy, lad."

Jack ran to the barn and came back with two slats of wood to support the tongue, and the repair job began. George Ingram and Will held the tongue in place as Father tried to attach it to a strong piece of cedar.

"You got scythes?" Samuel Dale asked.

"In the tool shed," Jack grumbled. "But what use are they?"

"I done it by hand before and I can do it again." Samuel headed for the barn.

"You'll have some time feeding the threshing machine with swathed grain," Jack said. But Samuel kept right on going with long, firm strides.

****

By twelve o'clock all the men were hot and grumpy and only too glad to be at the house for a full dinner. Nellie and Hannah had come back to the house a couple of hours earlier. And now they were in the kitchen with Mrs. Burnett, cooking up pork, potatoes, wild turkey, and carrots for the men.

Mother had set up two stools outside the back

kitchen door with basins of water and fresh towels, and the men stood in line waiting their turn to wash up. They could not go into Mrs. Mooney's house with dirty hands. But they did not wash their faces, for the chaff from the wheat being threshed in the afternoon would cut into their skin if it was washed. The men who had worked nearest the machine at the Ingrams' earlier that morning looked out through a mask of dust and dirt.

"Well, so much for finishing your wheat field today," said George as the men moved into the Mooney's big kitchen. "We'll have to start working on the stack by the barn, I'm afraid."

"No, George, we'll come close to finishing the field tonight. Lettie and the girls can do the evening barn chores. We just can't lose that crop."

"All right, then," said George. "I'll send Bert and Bob over after we finish our chores. I'm sorry I can't come, too, but I've got to attend to my grain." Father understood, for the threshing had just finished at the Ingrams, and as usual the men carrying away the bags of fresh wheat had not been able to keep up with the good yield. There would still be nearly fifty bags of grain waiting for George to empty into his granary bins.

As the men took their seats, Nellie started setting big bowls of mashed potatoes and creamed carrots on the table.

"You certainly know how to get a job done, Nellie L.," said Mrs. Burnett, who was ladling more potatoes into another bowl. "Not like that fool binder company that's giving us so much trouble. They made a lot of money out of us and they've taken no responsibility for their shoddy work."

She handed Nellie another bowl of mashed potatoes and creamed carrots. "I say the farmers should unite and make a formal complaint. And they should set their own grain prices, too. They've been pushed around long enough. Just look at the way the Conservative government in Ottawa is bossing us . . . Here, try some of Lettie's chili sauce, Frank. Ottawa promised Grand Valley they'd get the railway, and then at the very last minute they changed their minds."

"The government must have had a reason," Mother said as she handed Mrs. Burnett a platterful of huge pieces of fried side pork.

Mrs. Burnett took the plate over to the table and reached around her husband to set it down. Then she went back to the sideboard where Nellie's mother was pouring a pot-roasted wild turkey covered with fluffy dumplings and gravy into a huge bowl.

"Oh, they had a reason all right," said Mrs. Burnett as she waited for the bowl. "Land was cheaper around Brandon, so they moved the railway there. And they didn't care two hoots about all the people who moved to Grand Valley because they thought the railway was coming. Letitia, it's time women had a say in these matters."

Nellie saw her mother's mouth tighten into a fine line as she handed the bowl to Mrs. Burnett. "If the men can't make matters better, there certainly isn't any point in women trying."

"Well, if I weren't so busy making meals and baking, I'd think of a few ways to improve things. Maybe you girls will have time when you grow up." Mrs. Burnett set the bowl on the table and came back to the cupboard. She picked up a knife and started dishing pie onto the tea plates that Nellie had set out — one piece of raisin and one piece of cranberry for each of the men.

Lizzie was busy serving tea while Hannah stared in silence at Mrs. Burnett. Then Nellie said, "I'd like to try,

Mrs. Burnett." She was now refilling the vegetable bowls and pickle jars. "Women have lots of good ideas about how to manage things!"

"Nellie, you'll keep your comments to yourself. Now hurry up with those bowls and start helping Lizzie serve the tea. These men are parched."

Mrs. Burnett took some freshly baked buns from the oven and set them on the table. "Well, I told my Frank when he voted for the Conservatives, it was a mistake. Didn't I, Frank? But he voted Conservative anyway."

"Well, you could have just voted Liberal and cancelled out his vote," Nellie suggested.

"That's where you're dead wrong, child. Women don't have the vote. Didn't you know that, Nell?"

"I train my daughters to be good housekeepers," Mother said sternly. "And I don't let them concern themselves with matters men should handle."

"Well, why couldn't women be in government?" Nellie said. "We do all sorts of things around the farm. And we have to be smart to take care of things around the house. Mother is smart anyway. I think she'd be a very good prime minister." And, Nellie thought, a woman prime minister might do something to help the poor farmers' wives.

"Nellie Mooney, I will not listen to such talk in my kitchen. Now go outside and feed Nancy. Then, if you've learned to hold your tongue, you can come inside and help with the washing up."

Nellie walked out into the golden afternoon. Why, she thought, if Mother was such a good mother, did she know exactly how to make her daughter miserable? The day would come, she vowed, when Mother would not be able to tell her what she could and could not say. Mother would *not* keep her back forever.

Part Two

School Days

6

Nellie woke up with an overwhelming feeling of dread. The worst had come. It was October 15, 1883, the first day of school. She put her wrist to her forehead, hoping to feel a fever. No luck. "Well," she thought, "there's nothing for it but to face the thing squarely. Sooner or later, the world will have to find out that I don't even know how to read."

Her mother's words to Mrs. Ingram rang in Nellie's ears. "Nellie's a big girl — almost ten — and she won't learn anything!" She buried her head in the big feather pillow and tried to drown out the memory.

Mrs Ingram had smiled sympathetically and said, "Don't worry, Letitia. One of these days, she'll be able to read just like Bob!" Well, Bob Ingram was the last person Nellie wanted to be like, and he was the last person she wanted to see this morning.

Nellie turned over under the covers, then peeked

out at the bed beside her. For years, Nellie had been trying to figure out how Hannah managed to make her bed so there wasn't even the faintest wrinkle in the covers. Nellie's always had a lump or a ridge somewhere, even when she tried her hardest to pull the covers tight. And whenever she got rid of one lump, another would appear somewhere else as if by magic.

To Nellie's surprise, however, there was not only a wrinkle in Hannah's covers, there was a huge lump, too, and the lump was Hannah. Her auburn hair was just showing from under the blankets, and she was fast asleep. Hannah, the ever-sensible and almost perfect Hannah, was sleeping in on the first day of school! Nellie could not contain herself.

"Hannah, wake up. It's time for school!"

There was no response.

"Hannah . . . what's the matter with you? You have to go to school with me!" Nellie was starting to panic. She put one toe out onto the freezing floor. Now that harvest season was over, the mornings were icy.

"Hannah, don't play games with me. This is serious," Nellie said, now hanging over her sister with real concern and pushing her not too gently on the shoulder. Hannah stirred a bit, then woke up and started coughing.

"Nellie . . . I-I'm sick . . ."

Nellie's heart sank. If Hannah said she was sick, she really was, and that meant Nellie was on her own.

There was only one consolation, and that was the dress lying on the chair by the window. Nellie gazed at it lovingly as she shivered over to the washstand. It was grey homespun with small red checks and a white lace frill at the neck so the flannel wouldn't scratch. Lizzie had made it for her. There were light brown hand-knit stockings to go with it. Nellie might not know much about books, but she could at least go to school in that dress with her head held high, even if it was made of homespun instead of "store-bought" material.

Downstairs, Mother was stirring porridge over the fire and Jack was already finishing up his first bowlful.

"What are you staring at?" Jack mumbled.

"Nothing. What are *you* staring at?"

"If you look like that in school, the teacher'll make you sit in the corner with a dunce hat on."

"You're just jealous because you can't go."

"Jealous, hah!" Jack leaned his chair back and stuck his thumbs inside his suspenders. "You think I want to be cooped up at a desk all day with a teacher yelling at me? You must be daft. I've got a man's work to do here. We're ploughing all day today and Father can't do without me."

Mother interrupted as she ladled another serving of porridge into Jack's bowl. "As soon as the fall ploughing is done, you're going back to school, too. A few months in the winter won't hurt you. You only had five years of school back in Ontario."

Jack blushed and let his chair down with a thump. "That's as good as most boys my age or better . . . around here," he said, stuffing another spoonful of porridge into his mouth.

"Here's your bowl, Nellie. You'd better eat up — Hannah is too sick to go to school, so you're on your own. It's a good thing we already arranged for Bert and Bob Ingram to walk you over. They'll be coming any minute now."

Nellie started in on the porridge, but it tasted like sawdust.

It was lucky for Lizzie that she had completed her public school education in Ontario at age thirteen, as Mother needed her at home now. A cheerful helper, she came over from the stove with a heaping bowl of brown sausages and a plate of fried potatoes. Mother often said what a fine wife Lizzie would be one day. And the way Lizzie smiled at Mother's praise, Nellie knew that was exactly what Lizzie was hoping to be.

There was already a stack of fluffy pancakes on the table and a bowl of Mother's saskatoon-berry jam. But nothing appealed to Nellie. All she could think of was the terrible moment when the teacher would find out that she'd never learned to read.

"You look so smart in that dress, Nellie L.," Lizzie said, laying a fresh loaf of bread in front of Jack. "I am glad we decided on the lace around the collar. It makes you look like quite a lady."

That was just like Lizzie, Nellie thought. She always said something that made you feel better. But it couldn't last long on a day like today. She got up from the table without quite finishing her porridge and went to look out the window.

"You've hardly eaten enough to last a bird," Mother said.

"Oh, look, it's snowing," Nellie said, trying to distract her Mother from the subject of food. And it *was* snowing, too. Big, wet flakes were being driven down into the wheat stubble, and the sky was full of dark clouds.

Just then, the back door opened, and brushing snowflakes off their big coats, Will and Father stepped in from doing the morning chores.

"Sure, and it's winter already. I can feel that chill right to my bones. Letitia, you wouldn't have a cup of hot coffee for a freezing old farmer, would you? Ah, that smells good . . . Nellie, don't you look the lady today. I don't suppose you're going out to a dance."

"Oh, John, don't you put silly ideas into her head. She's going to school, of course."

"Ah, school, yes," said Father with a twinkle in his

eye. "Well, you'll be prettier than all the other girls, my Nellie L., with that dark brown hair of yours and that new dress." Father was like Lizzie, always trying to find the bright side, but she couldn't believe he liked her hair. It was just too terrible. It was shingled all the way up the back of her neck like the shortest boy's cut and could only hold a ribbon on the very top, which would look ridiculous. She could hardly stand to think about her hair.

"Now, Nellie, don't you worry about the teacher," Father went on. Nellie could never understand why, but her father always seemed to know what was bothering her without even asking. "I hear he's a very nice man who knows a lot but has even more patience than knowledge. He has a homestead over on Pelican Lake. His wife looks after the place during the week while he lives in the teacher's quarters, a small room back of the classroom. We're lucky to get him all the way up here."

There was a knock on the back door. Mother opened it, and in came Bob and Bert, with their hands over their ears and stamping their feet. Thank goodness Bert's going, too, Nellie thought. That way she wouldn't be stuck talking to Bob all the way to school. In school, Bob would have a chance to show off his reading every day. He was the last person she wanted to walk to school with.

Bob was dressed in another grey tweed suit, with knee pants and stockings and a short coat with pockets. It was obviously "store-boughten." A peashooter was sticking out of one of the pockets.

When they were on the road, Nellie asked Bob what the peashooter was for.

"Oh," he said, "a peashooter always comes in handy. If the teacher gives me any lip, I'll just sock him one." Nellie could hardly believe that was Bob talking. He was certainly brave about starting in at the new school. But then it was probably because he could read.

By the time they got to the school, which was two miles east of the farm, the snow had stopped falling, but gloomy, purple-blue clouds were glowering at them in the October sky. The three pupils hesitated at the firebreak — the six furrows that had been ploughed around the school yard to protect it against a prairie fire. There was no one outside the school. Classes must have already begun.

"I think we should just walk in," Nellie said. She wanted to get the thing over with as soon as possible.

"Don't you think we should knock first?" Bob asked.

Before Bert had a chance to add his opinion, the teacher rapped on the window and motioned them to come inside.

Bert, Nellie, and Bob walked into the one-room school, which still smelled of freshly cut wood. The teacher was sitting behind an unpainted desk.

"Good morning," he said, smiling at them, but his eyes were so bright and piercing, Nellie felt as if he was looking right through her. Maybe he could read her mind and already knew how ignorant she was.

"The older boy can take a seat over there," said the teacher, pointing to a desk by a window. "And you two, take your places in the middle of the third row."

Things were going from bad to worse. Bert could have helped Nellie a bit, but now he was way over on the other side of the room, and she'd have to sit beside the one person she couldn't stand to be near. Bob strutted to his seat and carefully put his armful of books and slate down on his desk. Nellie had no choice but to follow him, clutching her ragged Ontario reader, the one Hannah used to study from. She hid her slate under the reader because a bit had broken off the top and she didn't want anyone to see it.

She looked over at Bob. He was gazing at the teacher as if he were the prime minister. "Teacher's pet!" she thought.

Nellie slid as far as possible under the desk. Abigail Adams, who sat in front of her, had two thick golden braids hanging down her back. On the end of each was a big blue bow. Her dress was a beautiful shade of royal blue and was definitely made from store-bought cashmere. She wore a brilliant comb that exactly matched the two bows. And then there was her writing equipment. She had a slate with a red velvet border and a white cotton handkerchief with a herringboned hem, which she moistened in a little glass container before rubbing things off the slate.

The teacher cleared his throat. "Now, we'll tell each other our names in case someone doesn't know everyone. I'm Mr. Schultz, and I come from Pelican Lake. Now, you tell me your names, starting here." He motioned to the pupils at the desk just in front of him.

Nellie almost forgot her own name as the voices came closer to her. Finally there was dead silence. Abigail turned around and looked at her. Then everyone turned around and stared.

"Nellie Mooney," she heard Bob say. Giggles erupted from all corners of the classroom. Nellie was so embarrassed she just looked down at her broken slate.

"Now you may read your books or do some writing while I call you in turn to my desk to see what classes you'll be in. Be prepared to read something for me," the teacher said after everyone had been introduced.

Nellie pulled open her torn reader and stared at the marks inside. They started to go blurry, and her heart was beating faster. What was she going to say to the teacher?

"Abigail Adams, please," said Mr. Schultz. Nellie peeked up as Abigail and her bouncing bows left the seat in front of Nellie and started down the narrow aisle. She was carrying her fancy slate right up where everyone could see it. Nellie's stomach went all funny as she thought of her own bare neck and head and chipped slate. Someone was jabbing her in the ribs.

Bob was holding up his slate for her to see. She pushed him away. She didn't want to see his stupid writing. Then he jammed the slate right in front of her face. Nellie stared at it in disbelief. There was a picture of Mr. Schultz with a huge nose, and hair sticking out in all directions around his head. She nearly burst out laughing but grabbed her handkerchief from inside her sleeve just in time and pretended to blow her nose.

"Nellie Mooney," said the teacher. The dreaded moment had arrived. She pulled herself slowly out of her seat. Then she thought of something. She would count. She could not read, but thank goodness she could count to one hundred. She walked along the creaking floor. The whole class was probably staring at her, but she refused to look. She kept her eyes fixed on the teacher as she walked towards him.

Up close, he didn't look quite so bad. His eyes were actually grey with green flecks in them, and he was wearing a warm-looking brown knitted coat that had a pocket with a bit of a sag in it.

Nellie forgot all about her plan to count and blurted out, "I can't read. Hannah tried to teach me, but I can't even learn. And this Saturday, I'll be ten."

"That's a good age to start school," said Mr. Schultz, "and you'll be reading before Christmas break."

Nellie stared back at him. He hadn't scolded her for

being ignorant. But how could he be so sure she would be able to read before Christmas? All the same, there was something about the way he said it that made Nellie believe him. He looked steadily at her with his grey-green eyes. "You'll see," he said, and smiled kindly.

Nellie floated back to her seat. Her terrible burden had been lifted. She didn't care if Abigail had ten hundred different slate frames to match all her different store-bought dresses. And she didn't notice the neat sums that Bob had prepared as he slid out of his seat. All she knew was that she would be able to read by Christmas.

7

"I wish I could go back to school next week," Nellie complained to Will, who was sitting beside her in the sleigh.

"Well, that's a change of tune," he replied, smoothing the ends of his moustache and smiling out of the side of his mouth. "I seem to remember a little girl who lived here not long ago. I think she was going to be a cowboy, and she said she wouldn't need to read or go to school or anything."

"Oh, I gave that up weeks ago," Nellie said with confidence. "Mr. Schultz said I'd be able to read by Christmas. And it's only the second week in December and I can read! I'd rather be prime minister now, I think."

"Well, Madame Prime, how are you going to do that if women don't even have the vote?"

School had been closed for a week now because of bad weather, and Nellie and Will were on their way to

Millford to pick up the mail. Bert and Bob Ingram were in the back of the sleigh, sitting on the buffalo robe. It had been Will's idea to bring them along. Now that Nellie knew how to read, she didn't mind Bob so much, and she was glad of Will's idea. He knew how to make everything fun. Jack was just the opposite. All he knew was how to spoil everything.

Kate trotted bravely on beside the new horse, Duke, and their sleighbells jingled in the frozen air. Billy had died in August and been replaced by a strong young gelding.

Thank goodness for the sleighbells, Nellie thought. Jack had refused to come because of them. He thought they were sickening and sentimental. A man worth his salt would never drive with those things jangling in everyone's ears, Jack said. Nellie rather liked them. And she also liked the man who made them — their neighbour Tom Rae. No one was fooled by the gift. They knew Tom liked Lizzie and was trying to make a good impression on the family.

"Nellie — the prime minister! That'll be the day!" Bert laughed. Nellie turned around and gave him a cold stare. She didn't know Bert had been listening, and she thought he was more open-minded than that.

"Well, women should at least have the vote. You can't deny that," Nellie said.

"Oh, I don't know about that," Bert said. "We've done quite well without their vote. I don't see any reason to change the way things are."

"Well, I do. It's not fair."

Will looked fondly at his little sister. "Well, Nellie L., what's fairness got to do with anything? Life's often not fair, but we have to take things as they come. We . . ."

"I don't see what harm it could do to give women the

right to vote," Bob said. Bert gave his brother a patronizing stare. He knew Bob was trying to impress Nellie.

"Well, one thing is certain," Nellie said. "I am glad girls are allowed to learn to read. I would die now if I couldn't . . . Do you want to hear what we just learned in school?"

Before anyone could make an objection, she whipped out her reader and shouted above the sleighbells, "The snow had begun in the gloaming, and busily all the night had been heaping field and highway with silence deep and white."

"Yech," said Bob. "Will you stop being so sentimental? It's embarrassing." Bob had given up his readings and had been more interested in field hockey all fall.

****

At about noon, they pulled up to the post office, and Will got out and hitched up Kate and Duke. He put huge blankets on their backs to keep them warm. Beside them was an old horse without a blanket who looked something like Billy. He was stamping his feet and snorting, trying to stop shivering.

"Look at that, Will," said Nellie. "Don't you think we should put his blanket on him? He's freezing!"

"That he is," said Will, making a whistling sound through his front teeth. "I daresay his owner is off drinking at the bar. We call horses brutes, but look what liquor does to a man — makes him forget that someone is depending on him."

Bob and Bert looked around in the cutter for the poor horse's blanket, and were lucky to find it. It was hidden under a buffalo robe and looked all wrinkled — as if it had not been used recently. They threw the blanket over the animal and strode into the post office.

There was not much mail, but Will picked up the Mooneys' weekly *Family Herald,* the farmers' news magazine. Then they headed down to the general store to pick up sugar, flour, and salt along with some mustard for Lizzie's plaster. The whole family had come down with flu the first week of December, and Lizzie was still in bed with a heavy chest cold. Mother thought a mustard plaster would help.

In an hour they were back at the sleigh, getting ready to go home. "I'm glad you put the blanket on that poor skinny horse, Bob," Nellie said as she stared at a man weaving drunkenly towards the cutter next to them.

"It's what I thought," Will said grimly. "He's been in the tavern warming up and his animal has been outside freezing. Or would have been if we hadn't happened by. I hate to think what happens to that horse most of the time."

Nellie looked down into her lap and stroked the buffalo robe. She was thinking about Jed and how he was dead now because of a drunken man.

The horse owner had made his way to the cutter. He stumbled into the hitching post and fumbled at the reins. It took him a while, but he managed to untie the beast. Then he put one foot on the step of the cutter and tried to boost himself into his seat. But he kept losing his footing and slipping off the step. He nearly hit the ground a few times. Will was just about to get out of the Mooneys' sleigh when the man, puffing and red-faced, managed to heave himself into place.

The man pulled the big buffalo robe halfway across his lap and whipped the reins sharply across the horse's back. The horse spurted forward, but his blanket slid to the side and became entangled with the harness.

"My . . ." the man roared and pulled the reins tightly. The horse came to a sudden stop. The man stumbled out of the cutter and kicked the horse as he grabbed the blanket off. Then after repeated efforts, he made it back into his cutter.

Again the man lashed the reins across the horse's back. The cutter careened down the street with the man half bent over in the driver's seat.

Nellie vowed she would do something to stop the drinking that led to this cruelty. She had even heard of drunken men beating their wives the way this man had beaten his horse.

Beyond Millford, out in the open country, their mood changed a bit. It was difficult to remain sad for long in the bracing air. Every fence post and willow shrub was edged with hoar frost, and a bright blue sky stretched out over endless fields of glistening white. The runners sped over the hard drifts, and the jingle of the bells rang out sweetly in the clear air. The snow clipped up from the horses' hooves and bit like knives into Nellie's face.

Twenty minutes later, Will pulled the team to a stop for Bob and Bert to jump off the sleigh at the end of their lane.

"Thanks for the ride," Bert said as he and Bob reached for their supplies.

"Bye, Nell," said Bob. "I hope they open school soon."

They were off again. The Mooney home was just around the next turn.

"Is the new team faster?" asked Nellie.

"Well, I should say so. Duke has old Billy beat to pieces. Watch this!" Will slapped the horses across the back. They needed no further urging, for it was cold and they were in sight of their own warm barn.

As they entered the laneway, the horses were galloping at runaway speed. Then without warning, they turned into the barnyard before going to the house as Will had intended. The sleigh flipped sideways and straightened out again in seconds. Will clung to the reins and his seat, but Nellie rolled into a deep snowbank.

Snow was in her ears and mouth, but she soon scrambled to her feet, laughing. She had landed so lightly in the snow that she had enjoyed her tumble.

Nellie and Will were still laughing and brushing the snow off as they stumbled into the empty kitchen.

"Ho, there, anybody home?" Will shouted.

"The brave knights have returned with news from the outside world," Nellie announced.

The two messengers stopped dead. In their excitement they had failed to notice that the whole family was standing around the kitchen couch, where Lizzie was sleeping.

"Is she all right?" Will asked, walking over to the couch without taking his boots off. Mother looked up with a pained expression. She didn't even notice the puddles Will was making on the floor.

Nellie stayed at the door, afraid to move.

"She's taken a turn for the worse, Will. Now, did you get the mustard for the plaster?"

"Yes, Mother . . . it's here," said Will, setting his parcels on the table.

"Thank you, Will. Now, Nellie, help Hannah make supper. I can't leave Lizzie's side. She's a sick, sick girl."

Nellie whipped off her coat and walked over to the stove, where a big pot of soup was already boiling. As she worked on the rest of the meal, she could hardly smell the food. It was covered up by the odour of the turpentine and goose grease that Mother had rubbed on Lizzie's throat, chest, back, and sides. From time to time Lizzie would waken, and her thin shoulders shook from the hard, dry coughing.

"Please, God, make Lizzie better," Nellie prayed as she stirred the potatoes and chopped pork in the spider frying pan. "She's the best and kindest sister in the whole world."

****

At supper the family sat quietly around the table while Father thanked God for their meal and prayed for Lizzie. She had fallen into a fevered sleep but was not coughing as much now. They ate their meal without speaking; the only sound was the horrible rasp of Lizzie's heavy breathing.

After supper, Mother put the kettle on the stove and prepared mustard plasters with flour, dry mustard, and water. She wrapped the mixture into a piece of thin broadcloth and placed it on Lizzie's freshly rubbed chest and sides. The sick girl had sunk into a deep sleep.

"Lizzie . . . Lizzie," Mother said as she tried to rouse her to give her the medicine, but Lizzie did not waken.

As Nellie and Hannah slowly climbed the stairs to their bedroom, the sound of Lizzie's breathing became fainter. The two girls undressed as fast as they could and dived into bed to get warm. It was so cold they knew the water in the washstand pitcher would freeze to the bottom before morning. Weighted down with heavy quilts, they could hear only their own chattering teeth and the wind squealing around the eaves of the house.

"She'll be better in the morning," Hannah said. "You'll see." Nellie was not so sure, but she was glad to hear Hannah say it. She felt a little better as she drifted off to sleep.

A few hours later, Nellie woke with a start. She could

hear Hannah's gentle breathing near her, but she knew something was wrong. She threw back the covers and winced as her feet touched the cold mat. A moaning sound was coming from the kitchen. She tiptoed across the room and down the steep stairway.

She looked out into the room and drew back at the sight. There was Mother kneeling beside the kitchen couch in her nightgown with her long, dark hair loosened and falling down her back. "I'm beaten," she cried. "I can't save her. Please, please touch my little one with Thy healing hand. I can do no more." Then her shoulders shook with sobs as she buried her face in her hands on the sofa. Nellie turned away and climbed the stairs back to bed. Surely Lizzie would be better in the morning.

****

Nellie wakened to a silent day. The sky was still dim behind the frost-covered window, but the wind must have died down. She threw back the covers and donned her shirt and drawers, then pulled on her brown cambric work dress and crisp white apron and hurried down the stairs.

The table was set for breakfast, and Hannah was busy stirring oatmeal porridge in a big iron pot. Someone had hung quilts up around Lizzie's couch to keep her warmer. Mother stepped out from behind the quilts and sat down in the rocking chair beside the stove. As she rocked, she looked straight ahead. Her eyes looked almost sightless — like Lizzie's.

"Mother, Lizzie is getting better . . . isn't she?" Nellie asked. "Mother. . ." When Mother did not answer, Nellie looked at Hannah.

"Mother will have Lizzie better in no time," whispered

Hannah. "Now come, don't bother her. She's been up all night, and Father and the boys will soon be in from the chores and wanting breakfast ready . . . Here, slice this bread."

Nellie took the knife and sliced across the loaf as she stared at Mother, who was still rocking in the chair. She wished that Father would come in soon, for she could see the fear in her mother's eyes. Just then Mother turned to Nellie. "Heat the chicken broth. I'm going to try to give her some again. She's got to take something." Mother rushed over to the cupboard for a cup and spoon. Nellie set the pan of broth on the hottest part of the stove.

"Not too hot," said Mother. "She can't take it too hot." Nellie tried a spoonful herself and poured a little into the cup that Mother held out.

"Hold back the quilts, please, Nellie," said Mother. "Maybe she needs a little more air."

Nellie opened the quilts and gazed down at Lizzie. Her eyes were open, but they were clouded over and she was staring straight ahead without sight. Her face was stone-white. Mother put the spoon to Lizzie's lips, but the broth just ran back down her chin. Her breathing was still heavy and she hesitated between each breath.

Mother bowed her head, put the spoon back in the cup, and got up. She motioned Nellie to leave, then stepped outside the quilt curtain herself.

Father, Will, and Jack came in from the barn at that moment, stamping the snow from their boots. Father hurried to close the door behind them, then walked over to the stove, where his sons were already warming their hands.

Mother, still rocking, gave a low sob. "My little girl is dying," Mother gasped. "If only we weren't eighty miles to a doctor. He could drain the fluid from her lungs, but I can't. John, we never should have come . . . It's tearing my heart out to see my little girl die before my eyes . . . What's money? What's land? What comfort can we have when we remember this — our child dying for want of a skilled hand — the best child I ever had."

Father spoke then. "You've done the best you could, Lettie. But you've always said while there's breath, there's hope. So don't give up. You're exhausted just now, from not getting enough sleep . . . You'll see, she may pull through yet."

"She's such a good girl . . . such a willing helper . . . the best child a mother ever had," said Mother. She rocked back and forth now with her hands clutching the sides of the chair.

Nellie could not stand to stay in the house anymore. She walked to the back door, grabbed her coat, hat, and mitts from the nail and quietly stepped outside. She would go to the barn.

Outside the house, all colour dissolved into whiteness and every sound was drowned out by the wind. The storm was wild again, and the cold air hit her face like a raw whip. The stinging pain seemed to give her some relief from the mental anguish. For once, the howling of the wind was welcome. She would face it bravely. She could face anything but the pain of seeing Lizzie die. She gripped the rope that ran between the house and the barn and waited for the storm to let up a bit.

But the snow kept on rolling in with the wind. It lashed Nellie again with its rawness. She could see that it was not going to stop, so she started out for the barn, holding the guideline firmly with one hand.

Inside the barn, the moist warmth from the animals soothed her stinging face and hands. But the sound of their contented chewing seemed distant as she stumbled over to the stone landing between the cow mangers. Nap was there, curled up on a pile of hay her brothers had thrown down for the cows' breakfast. She sank down beside him on the hay and stared blankly ahead. When Nap realized she was there, he lifted his head and licked her face. Nellie put both arms around him and buried her forehead in his thick, furry coat. The tears streamed down her cheeks.

She did not know how long she sat there, but when the howling wind roused her at last, she knew she should go back to the house. People would be wondering where she'd gone. She pushed Nap away slowly, brushed the hay from her clothes, and with one mitten wiped the tears away from her cheeks.

As she stepped out of the barn, a gust of wind and snow blew her back, but she struggled against it and grabbed the rope. Then she launched out into the whiteness. She had gone only about ten feet when the wind suddenly died down. A hundred feet ahead of her, down by the creek, she thought she saw someone approaching. It was a man in a big raccoon coat, snowshoeing up the hill. Nellie turned and ran to the house.

"Someone's coming," she shouted as she entered the kitchen.

"Are you sure, Nellie?" Father said in a tired voice.

"Yes, look! It's a man on snowshoes!"

A few minutes later, the man came to the door and stepped into the kitchen. It was Thomas Hall, the Methodist minister from Millford. He set a small snow-covered bag on the floor and handed Father his snowy coat. "I'm making the rounds visiting, and what a day to pick! It wasn't that bad when I started out," he said and hesitated at the sound of Lizzie's harsh breathing. "There's been a lot of sickness. I've brought medicine that just came in from Brandon. Some for this flu that's been going around."

Across the room, Mother stopped her rocking and looked up, "God must have sent you," she said. She drew back the curtains from Lizzie, who was still staring blankly. Mr. Hall knelt by her bed and lifted one thin, little hand and felt for her pulse.

8

Nellie lay stretched out in the pasture, staring straight up at the clouds travelling lazily across the June sky. Nap sat beside her, keeping an eye on the cows. Six months had passed since Lizzie's illness. The minister's medicine had worked, and Lizzie was back on her feet in time for Christmas. Nellie smiled as she remembered the first day Lizzie was able to get out of bed. A few weeks before, no one would have believed she would live.

Nellie's smile faded as she remembered why she was lying in the open pasture. The cows had stripped all the goosegrass and prairie hay in the Mooneys' small fenced pasture, so now they had to be grazed out in the open. It was Nellie's job to make sure they didn't stray into the grainfields and eat the new shoots of wheat.

A year ago Nellie would have been happy to have this job. But now the thing she wanted most was to go to school. It had broken her heart to see Hannah and Bert and Bob Ingram heading up the trail to Northfield School that morning.

Unfortunately, Nellie was the only one who could mind the cows. Father needed Jack's help in the fields and Mother needed Lizzie in the house. Hannah was the smartest student in the whole school, according to Mr. Schultz, and could not be held back. She would soon be ready to go to Winnipeg to study for her teaching certificate. Will couldn't help either. He had built a cabin on his own place now and was busy with his work.

Sometimes Nellie felt like drowning the cows. If it weren't for them, she wouldn't be held prisoner like this. To make matters worse, a drought had hit the West and all the farmers were in a bad mood. If no rain came, the young wheat shoots would just shrivel up, and there would be no crop.

"Oh, well," Nellie sighed. "This is the life of the peasants, and I'll just have to put up with it, won't I, Nap?" Nap opened his mouth, yawned, and nodded his head.

Nellie rolled over onto her stomach and opened her Collier's History. Her class was studying about King John and his nobles and how they battled at Runnymede. She wondered what the peasants had been doing at that time. Probably they just went on raising their crops and watching their cows. That was the fate of the common people.

"Well, I'm not going to suffer that fate," she thought. "I'm going to get a teaching certificate like Hannah and escape from the farm."

Nellie was jolted out of her dreaming by the sound of Nap barking. But there were other sounds, too — a throaty, unfamiliar bark, louder than Nap's, and the bellowing of cattle. Nellie sprang to her feet. The cattle were rushing up the other side of the creek with Nap and the neighbours' dog, Wolf, yapping at their legs. Wolf was a mean dog who had caught a lot of wolves. The whole neighbourhood knew that Mr. Brown kept the vicious animal just so he could get the wolf bounties.

Nellie ran down the knoll to the creek and splashed into the water. If only she could reach them before it was too late. Then she heard frenzied and painful bellows. Big mangy, liver-coloured Wolf was hanging from the tail of a two-year old heifer, who was running wildly ahead of the others. And Nap . . . Nap was swinging from the tail of the old black cow at the back of the bunch. Nap had never done such a thing before. Wolf must have taught him the nasty trick. Nellie hurled her brown history book at her dog; it hit him on the head, and he loosened his hold and fell to the ground.

"Bad dog," Nellie shrieked as she raced beyond him towards Wolf. She snapped her switch — a soft maple sapling — and missed. But he turned then and ran, disappearing in the direction of home to the west. The cows were panting, terrified. The heifer continued to bellow and ran from Nellie when she ran to her side.

Nellie touched the rumps of three cows with her switch and prodded them back to the creek. Nap slunk along beside her, sorry now for what he had done. But Nellie knew he was doomed, for he had snapped off two cows' tails before. Father had said that if it happened one more time, it would be the last. No farmer could afford a dog that hurt cattle and lowered their market price. When a regular tail with its hairy switch hit a milker's head, it was bad enough, but the clout of a bony bobtail was a heavy blow. No one wanted bobtail cows.

The big heifer was standing quietly by the creek, and Nellie ran up to her. Tearing a strip off her petticoat, she dipped it into the water and squeezed it onto the red wound. When the cow did not move, she gently bathed the bloody mess of bone and skin. Nap's teeth marks were deep in the bone, but the tail had not been cut right off. It was hanging on by a thread. Nellie wrapped the white strip around the wound to hold the tail in place.

Then she turned to the other cow, who was at the far end of the herd, still bawling in pain. As Nellie stepped silently up beside her, the cow raced away. The switch of her tail was hanging down limp. It would be useless to follow her while she was still so scared.

Nellie turned and walked up the hill to where Nap was sitting, spattered with cow's blood. "Bad dog! Bad dog!" she yelled and raised her maple switch. Nap drew his ears flat against his head and waited for his punishment. She raised her stick but could not bring herself to hit a dog who was about to be shot.

"Come on, Nap, let's wash you off in the creek." She tried to make her voice sound mean. Nap went to lick her hand, but she drew it back. Cow's blood was still oozing from his mouth.

Nellie knelt beside him at the water's edge and with another strip from her petticoat washed away every sign of his guilt.

Her task completed, Nellie started trudging up the knoll but found she could go only a few steps. She dropped to her knees, sprawled out on the ground, and burst into sobs. Nap sniffed at her neck, and the cows gathered in a circle around her, staring at the small, shaking body.

As she was crying, Nellie suddenly remembered some healing salve that her father kept in the barn for emergencies. It was Balm of Gilead that Mother had made from buds in the spring. It might help the tails to heal.

She raced back to the creek, splashed through it, and climbed up the other side, towards the barn.

As she burst through the cowstable door, Nellie was taken aback by the sight of her father. He was almost always out in the fields at this time of day.

"Whatever's the matter, Nellie?" he said, raising his eyebrows.

"It's that miserable dog, Wolf. He's been after the cows' tails again," Nellie blurted out. Father could see that her face was all splattered with blood and stained with tears.

"Did he get you, Nellie?"

"No, no. I'm fine and I tried to bind up their tails. But the heifer wouldn't let me touch her. I thought Mother's Balm of Gilead might help."

Father shook his head. "Which ones were bit?"

"The two-year-old heifer and Blossom."

"Here's the salve, but I'm going with you." Together they stepped back out into the bright day and hurried along the path to the creek.

When they reached the cattle, Father examined the black cow first. He took off the binding, rubbed in the salve, and rewound the homemade bandage. "You've done a good job, Nellie L. I couldn't have done any better myself. Now let's corner the heifer."

The young cow was pacing a few feet away from the others now and thrashing her wounded tail about. The hairy switch hung sideways from the bone.

"Co-boss . . . there, co-boss," Father said in a firm, quiet voice. The heifer turned her big pleading eyes on him, but Father kept going towards her. "Quick, Nellie, wet this cloth," he said, holding out a piece of an old shirt he'd carried from the barn. He rubbed the cow's back as he waited.

Nellie dipped the shirt in the cool creek water, ran

back up the hill, and handed it to Father. He squeezed the water from the towel, then rubbed it gently against the wound. Once the chunks of blood were cleared away, it was easy to see that the tail had been cut away from the hairy switch. It was held together only by a thin piece of skin.

"I doubt it'll grow, but I'll give it a chance," Father said. "Here, Nellie, hold the switch to the bone while I bind them together." Father covered the rag with Balm of Gilead and wound it tightly around the wound. "She'll probably lose it, but it's worth a try. Sometimes they grow back together in the younger ones."

As they headed back to the house, Father was grumbling. "I don't know why they keep that low-bred cur. He should have been shot last spring when he took the tail off the Ingrams' young heifer."

The guilty Nap was trotting along beside them, looking as innocent as a puppy. There were no telltale splotches of blood on his furry coat or around his mouth. Nellie had done a good job of washing him.

"Father," she said, and tears flooded from her eyes. "I have something . . ."

Father reached down and took Nellie's hand in his big one. "It's all right now, Nellie L. Don't worry about it. It's not your fault. and I don't think the black cow will lose her tail . . . maybe not even the heifer." They walked up the knoll to the house in silence.

It was the black cow, Blossom, that Nap had bitten, Nellie reasoned, and if the black cow wasn't going to lose its tail, then why did she need to say anything?

At the supper table, Jack tried to poke holes in her story. "I'm surprised Nap wasn't involved." He shot Nellie a sharp glance, but she was reaching for the potato bowl and did not look at him. "He's snapped tails before and he might do it again."

The potato bowl hit the table with a clatter. "Why do you always have to say mean things, Jack?" she screamed.

"I was right then. Nap is guilty, too. I can see you're hiding something, so don't deny it. Everyone knows you'd lie to save Nap."

"Jack! That's enough," Mother interrupted. "No one in this whole neighbourhood would doubt Nellie's word. That's a terrible thing to say. Tell your sister you're sorry — right this minute."

"Sorry," Jack mumbled across the table, but he was still staring at Nellie as she choked down her food.

After supper, Nellie went to bed early. Everyone knew she was still upset about the cows, so they were not surprised. But she only pretended to be asleep when Lizzie and Hannah came quietly upstairs and crawled into bed without a light so they wouldn't disturb her. Nellie lay there in a cold sweat. Finally she heard the sound of her sisters' soft breathing as they slept, but all she could think of was how she had lied to save Nap. No one would question her further now that Mother was on her side, but Nellie kept squirming beneath the quilts. Surely God knew and would punish her.

The family had prayed every day for rain for the pasture and the crops, but now God might not let it rain all summer. They would have the worst drought possible, and it would be all her fault. She tossed about in her feather bed far into the night.

Still awake in the early hours of the morning, she heard a tinkling that sounded like rain on the roof. She could not believe her ears. It really was raining and it was coming down harder all the time. Nellie turned over and fell asleep with a bit of a smile on her face.

9

"There's always the danger of frost," Will said as he gulped down the pancakes that Mother had just put on his plate. It was September, and the Mooney men were still working on the harvest.

"It's too soon for frost, Will," Father said, smiling at Mother as she handed him a plate of fried potatoes and eggs. He had already been up for two hours, milking the cattle and cleaning out their stalls. Though he was sixty-nine years old, he was still strong and able to work as long a day as the boys.

"The harvest would be in already if that miserable binder hadn't broken down again," Jack grumbled.

"Well, no use crying over spilt milk," Father said. "We just need to keep going. If it weren't for this rheumatism in my knees, I could go all day and all night, too. Jack, pass little Nellie the toast. She'll be busy today . . . back at school."

Nellie could hardly wait to be off, even though Mother was making her wear homemade red bloomers. They were the most awful-looking things. This was not surprising, since they had originally been Mother's nightgowns. She had dyed them red to make a mat. Then, to save money, she had decided to use the material to make Nellie's underclothes. There was no money to buy new clothes these days — not until the grain was sold, and maybe not even then.

Nellie and Hannah finished their breakfast, gathered up their books, and headed off for school. Nellie walked carefully beside her sister, trying to make sure her dreadful bloomers didn't show. She felt safe with Hannah, who knew just about everything, it seemed. This would be Hannah's last year at Northfield School. She would be going to study for her teacher's certificate next fall.

Nellie was about to start reciting her memory work to Hannah when they arrived at the Ingrams. Bob had grown over the summer and was now taller than Nellie, even though he was still ten and she was nearly eleven. Bert was home helping with the harvest. As the three of them walked along the prairie towards the school, they could feel the grass soft beneath their feet. The sky was a cloudless blue and the Tiger hills were a beautiful mauve in the distance.

"Bert's hoping the binder doesn't break down, and we'll soon be ready for the threshers," said Bob.

"Yes, our binder's been giving trouble again, too." Hannah sighed. "Jack never seems to get used to that. He's in a terrible bad mood all the time now."

"I wonder what grade I'll be in," Nellie said. "I was in third grade with Abigail in June, but she's probably passed into fourth grade by now."

Bob shifted his books to his other arm. "I bet you

won't be behind for long, Nellie. Who else ever got into Grade Three in their first year? You'll do all right."

Nellie smiled at Bob. He was improving.

****

Two weeks later Nellie was sitting in at recess to work on her history studies. Mr. Schultz had put her into the fourth grade with Abigail, and the work was not easy. But just this morning, for the first time ever, she had moved into first place with the top mark in reading.

Turning the page in her reader, Nellie looked up as Abigail brushed by her desk. "Nellie, why don't you come out and play shinny?" she asked in a sweet tone — too sweet.

"Because I'm busy doing better things."

"Oh, really. Isn't it because you don't want anyone to see your red bloomers?" Nellie looked up in shock. She hadn't thought anyone besides her sister knew about those bloomers, and she knew Hannah would never tell anyone.

Abigail continued. "I only let you beat me at reading this morning because I feel sorry for you. Everyone knows you only have one dress you wear to school every single day. And besides, you can't crochet or do needlework like the rest of us." With that, Abigail whipped around and marched out the door.

Nellie was furious. She would get even with Abigail and the crochet squad.

****

On the way home from school that day, Nellie had to admit to Hannah that she was a bit jealous of how all the other girls could crochet. And that night, she tried out a simple pattern that Lizzie gave her. She sat in the rocking chair by the stove knotting and twisting for two hours. She even stuck her tongue out slightly while she was doing it — a sign of great concentration. But she just could not get the right crook in her little finger.

"What are you trying to do, Nellie L.," Lizzie said at last, raising her eyebrows and trying not to giggle. She'd been watching her frantic efforts and trying not to interrupt.

"It's no use, Lizzie," Nellie said, throwing down the hook and yarn, which was now all dirty from being held tightly for two hours. "I hereby renounce all handiwork. There's only one thing I can do and that's reading and schoolwork. I can't even do the mile-a-minute pattern. And everyone can do that one — even Abigail Adams' little sister, Maude!"

****

The next day, Nellie was firmer than ever in her resolve to throw herself into her homework. She stayed in at recess and applied herself to her history lesson. Then at noon, she had a brilliant idea. It was Friday, the day that Mr. Schultz always asked the pupils to read their own stories and poems. She would write a poem about the virtues of studying and read it to the class. That would teach the crochet squad a thing or two.

Reading time came and Nellie stood up in the aisle beside her seat to recite her invention:

> The heights of great men reached and kept
> Were not attained by sudden flight,
> But they, while their companions slept,
> Were toiling upward in the night.
> They did not leave their reading books

To fool around with crochet hooks;
They did not slight their history notes
To make lace for their petticoats;
But step by step they did advance
And gave no thought to coat or pants!
So let my steps be ever led
Away from wool, and crochet thread;
So let my heart be set to find
The higher treasures of the mind.

"Thank you, Nellie Mooney," said Mr. Schultz. "A fine poem, with a little help from Longfellow."

Nellie sat down, feeling victorious, although she had to admit the poem was not quite original.

If she thought she had got the message across, however, she was sadly mistaken. After school, as she and Hannah and Bob were walking down the front steps, Maude Adams stopped her and looked up at her with eyes full of sympathy. "You know, Nellie Mooney, you don't need to feel bad the way the person in the poem did. You aren't the only one who can't do crochet work. My mother knows this grown lady who can't. Mother says she can't help it. It's because her mother and father are cousins."

Nellie looked at Maude and sighed. "Thanks, dear," she said. Nellie ran to catch up with Hannah and Bob.

"Did you like my poem?"

"Well . . ." said Hannah, "it was good, but . . . just a bit spiteful, maybe. Just because you can't crochet doesn't mean you should make fun of those who can."

"Well, I was tired of being made fun of. And I'm tired of doing farmwork and housework all the time. Reading books is much more interesting."

"But Nellie, if you ever want to marry, you'll have to learn to do housework and farmwork because women are expected to keep their households going. There's just no time to sit and read on a farm."

****

"Hello, Father," Nellie shouted as she and Hannah turned into their laneway. He was returning from the Ingrams' threshing, driving a team with an empty wagon. He stopped as he came up to the two girls.

"Have you seen Nap on your way home from school?" he asked.

"No. Why?"

Father looked worried. "Frank Burnett said he saw him fighting with the Ingrams' boar this afternoon. He said he was wounded. Frank couldn't stop because he was bringing water for the boiler on the threshing machine, and he couldn't keep the men waiting. I couldn't leave either. I was busy hauling grain to the granary all afternoon. And I can't go after him now. I have to get right back there."

Nellie ran into the house, dropped her books, and raced back down the road towards the Ingrams, where Nap had last been seen. She kept pulling back bushes along the road as she went until she had almost reached the Ingrams' laneway.

Bob came running from the house. "What are you doing back here, Nellie?" he asked. "I could see you from the kitchen window . . . You look white as a ghost!"

"It's Nap. We think he fought with your boar, and he's wounded. Maybe he's even crawled away somewhere to die," she gulped out as she tried to hold back her tears. Maybe this was God punishing her for lying about the cows' tails. She had thought that God had forgotten all about it by now, but maybe he hadn't.

"Nap may still be alive. He wanders over here sometimes. He's probably chasing a groundhog."

"He'd be home by now. He's always there at suppertime."

"Let's keep looking, then," he said. "If he were wounded, I think he'd try to make it home. Let's start back towards your place."

They left the main road and ran across ploughed fields, looking for any sign of torn ground or black hair and blood. "Here, Nap! . . . Oh, Nap!" Nellie called over and over again, then listened for an answer. But she could hear nothing.

They began to retrace their steps and had not gone far when Nellie saw something in the bushes near the creek. "Please, God, let it be Nap," she breathed to herself. And it was Nap, though he didn't look much like himself. He was just a still mass of blood-stained fur.

Nellie dropped to her knees beside him. He was alive, but now she saw that he was bleeding from a great hole in his chest. He tried to lift his head when he saw Nellie. But he had barely raised it from the ground before he let it sink back again.

"Quick, get some flour from Mother to stop the bleeding," said Nellie. Bob started off. "And bring a towel, too."

Bob came back in a few minutes. Nellie dropped big handfuls of flour into the wound and wrapped the towel tightly around his chest before Bob offered her the sack he had brought. "If we put him on this bag, we'll be able to carry him to the barn."

As they pulled him along, Bob said, "Don't give up, Nellie. As long as a dog is breathing, there's hope."

"Let's put him in the woodhouse. It's warmer there." They opened the woodhouse door and lifted Nap up over the doorsill. He whimpered in pain but still did not move. Nellie piled together a few old sacks, and they laid him down on them.

"I'll go for some milk," Bob suggested. "It might give him some strength." Nellie nodded, and Bob hurried out the door.

"I'll stay with you, Nap," Nellie said, trying not to cry. The dog tried to lift his head, then lay still again.

When Bob came back, Nellie put a little milk in her hand and tried to get Nap to lick her fingers, but he could not move. Nellie sat back and leaned her head against the wall in despair.

"It's no use," Nellie said in a low voice. "You might as well go home. You've been a big help, but I don't need you now."

"Goodbye, Nellie. I hope he's better in the morning."

Nellie sat half-crouched over the dog. Is this what Nap gets because I lied to save him? It would have been better if Father had shot him. There would have been no fear, no bleeding, no agony like this — only a sudden shot and his life would have been over.

Nellie's thoughts were interrupted by Jack, who had flung open the woodshed door. "Mother says you better come in for supper."

"I can't eat."

"He probably would have died soon anyway, Nellie. We both know about his habit of snapping cows' tails," Jack said. Nellie thought he was being mean, but his voice was kind.

In a few minutes, Jack was back, holding out a glass of milk to Nellie. "Mother says you're to drink this." On his other arm, he had an old coat. Nellie took it and laid it over Nap. "He'll need to keep warm," Jack said. "He's lost a lot of blood. Mother's heating hot bricks to put beside him."

Nellie huddled a bit closer to Nap as Jack walked out and shut the door. It was dark and quiet inside, and Nap's breathing could barely be heard.

After supper Mother came out with a small bowl of warmed milk and two heated bricks inside socks. She tried to give Nap a little milk on a spoon, but most of it trickled down his jaw. Mother shook her head sadly. "If he's still alive in the morning, we'll wash his wounds and put some Balm of Gilead on them, but for now, I think it's best we leave him alone. You come along to bed now."

"I'll come soon," Nellie said, but she knew she would not leave him. She would stay beside him all night. As she sat in the darkness, she remembered how she had carried him around proudly in a basket that first summer. And she was going to miss racing through the fields for the cows with him. Most of all, she would always be thankful to him for guarding the henhouse door. "I'll never forget you, Nap," she sobbed, gazing at her bleeding friend.

She dragged over a few empty sacks from the far corner of the shed and put them down beside Nap. She laid her head on the sacks, still looking at the dog, who was lying as silently as before. Before long, she fell asleep.

10

When Nellie woke up, the grey light of dawn was coming in through the small window in the shed and a pile of wood loomed before her. Then she remembered where she was, and she looked over at Nap, who was lying a couple of feet away. He was breathing still, but his eyes were glazed over.

Nellie struggled to her feet, smoothed out her dress, and ran to the kitchen. She put a few sticks of kindling into the stove and lighted it. About twenty minutes later, a good fire was crackling. Just then Mother came out of the bedroom. "You're up — ahead of me!" she said. She picked up the old iron pot, put it on the stove, and poured in some dry oatmeal and water. Hot porridge would soon be simmering there for the family.

"How's Nap?" she asked as she stirred the porridge.

"He's the same," Nellie mumbled.

"Well, I'll go take a look at him after I have breakfast ready."

Nellie gazed at her Mother and felt as if she did love her after all. Her face was so comforting as she bent over the stove, as she did every morning at this time. Nellie knew that in a few minutes she would have to go out to help milk the cows. The work would continue as always — even if Nap was struggling for his life. And Nellie was glad there was work to do, for she could not bear to sit and watch Nap any longer. In that grey dawn she realized that the daily routine must go on and would go on . . . whether Nap lived or not.

****

The next day Nellie slouched in her seat between Mother and Hannah in the church pew as the Reverend Mr. Hall delivered his Sunday morning message. It was a balmy September day — much milder than usual — and only a light breeze came through the open window into the one-room church in Millford. The congregation was small — about fifty people — but it seemed almost crowded in the little building. Lizzie sat just across the end of the aisle with Tom Rae, who called on her regularly now and drove her to church every Sunday.

Nellie looked out the open window past Father and Jack, who were sitting at the other end of the family pew. She was thinking only of Nap. He had lived all through yesterday, and this morning Mother had washed his wound and said there was some hope. But Nellie was not comforted. She had an overwhelming feeling of remorse, for she knew it was her own fault. God was punishing her for lying about Nap.

God had not denied the rain, for that would have

hurt the whole family, but now he was punishing just her and Nap. She couldn't tell anyone. Mother would never believe anything she said again if she confessed, and she could not let Mother down. One thing was certain. She would never tell another lie. She had learned her lesson, but she must bear the guilt of this lie . . . to her grave.

They would bury Nap in the backyard, Nellie decided. She would see that he had a proper gravestone. Maybe Will could drag a huge stone to the spot on his wooden stoneboat. With a nail, she would scratch a fitting verse on the stone.

Nap Mooney — Beloved dog of my life,

Braver than all dogs before,
Met his end in strife,
With a willful boar,
And uttered his last groan,
When all alone,
While the family sat in church.

A tear slid down Nellie's cheek as she thought of it. Maybe even now Nap was groaning weakly and going into dog heaven or wherever it was that dogs went.

Nellie's gloomy thoughts were rudely interrupted by the minister's voice. "For without are dogs," he was saying. He was reading from the Book of Revelation — the part about the people who would be cast out from the heavenly city. Surely he must be talking about those dogs who bit cows' tails. Nellie sat up even straighter and strained to catch every word.

". . . and sorcerers, and whoremongers," read the minister. Nellie couldn't picture them, for she couldn't understand what the words meant.

". . . and murderers and idolaters." Nellie was sure she didn't know any of them.

". . . and whosoever loveth and maketh a lie."

Suddenly Nellie's heart sang for joy. She was not in that list, for though she had made a lie, she had not loved it! God, who knew everything, would know she had not loved it. She had lied because she couldn't help herself, but she had not loved it. God would understand, she decided, and if God understood, then what did she need to feel guilty for? She felt that God had forgiven her. But that did not mean that he would let Nap live. All the same, she would be able to stand it now if Nap died, since she knew God had forgiven her.

After the service, Nellie squirmed in behind a group of adults who were standing on the wooden stoop at the church entrance, waiting to shake hands with the minister. She rushed down the steps and went to sit in the wagon.

Finally Jack jumped into the wagon and sat beside Nellie, who stared straight ahead, ignoring him. "Well, I guess we should be getting home," he said. Nellie looked up in surprise. Why was he being so nice?

Without waiting for her answer, Jack was out of the wagon again and untying the team from the hitching post. He jumped in the front seat and turned the team around and drove them right up to the little crowd of people outside the church. Mother looked startled and a bit angry, but Father looked straight at Nellie. Then he took Mother's arm and started for the wagon.

"Come along, Lettie," Father said as he looked back over his shoulder. "We've a sick animal that needs checking on."

All the way home, dark clouds loomed on the horizon, and the harvested fields looked bare. There was a chill in the air that Nellie had not noticed on the way to town. She shivered and thought of poor Nap lying cold in the woodshed.

As Father turned into the lane, Nellie felt sick at heart again. But Father was being so kind. Before taking the horses to the barn, he headed right up to the house and stopped beside the woodshed. Nellie jumped down, ran to the door and swung it open. As her eyes adjusted to the darkness, she could see that Nap was still breathing.

"Nap . . . Nap," Nellie said, running over to him. She put her hand under his furry ear and could not believe it when he lifted his head up a bit. She patted the little black spot on his forehead, and he tried to lick her hand.

Nellie smiled with relief. Nap was going to make it after all. God had not only forgiven her. He had let Nap live.

11

"Nap, Nap, get away from that tree," Nellie shouted. "If you don't stop wagging your tail, you're going to knock it over."

The Mooney women and Mrs. Ingram were standing in the kitchen, washing up after Christmas dinner. Nap was walking around the front room, begging bits of cookies from the men and sniffing at the Christmas tree.

"Just think," said Mrs. Ingram, "one more week and it'll be 1885. That means we've been west almost five years now. It's hard to believe."

"Yes, things have changed a lot in a short time — but mostly for the better," said Mother, who looked younger this Christmas than she had in a long time.

"Yes, some things have changed, but the weather hasn't," Mrs. Ingram complained. "I've never yet eaten bread in the winter that wasn't frozen. Even when I wrap it in George's fur coat, it freezes!"

This Christmas had been the best one yet in the Mooney household. Will had cut a spruce tree from the sandhills on the road to Millford, and there were lots of boughs left over for decorating the windows and door-sills. The log walls of the front room had been white-washed, and there was a new mica-sided stove in the centre of the room to keep everyone warm.

This year, too, the Ingrams had come to share the turkey, apple-jelly tarts, and plum pudding. Mrs. Ingram wore a dolman of smoke-grey brocaded velvet and a black silk dress with a gold brooch set in pearls. Nellie thought she looked just like an elegant Montreal lady — the kind she'd seen in the *Family Herald Supplement.*

Nellie was actually rather proud of her own new green cashmere dress, even though it was now covered with a white apron.

Father and Mr. Ingram and the boys were sitting around the stove in the front room.

"They say Riel is back in Saskatchewan," Father said as the women came into the front room and sat down.

Mr. Ingram shook his head. "I can't understand why the government allows it. He's stirring up the half-breeds and Indians — and mark my words, there'll be trouble soon."

"Why don't they arrest him before someone gets killed?" Mother asked. When it was a matter of her family's safety, she didn't mind giving an opinion.

"Louis Riel has already killed one white man — Thomas Scott," said Mrs. Ingram. "Maybe he'll strike again. I'm just glad we don't live in Saskatchewan."

"The Redcoats should have moved in long ago," said

Mr. Ingram. "They should know who's in control here, anyway."

Nellie was trying not to say anything because she knew what Mother would think, but it was hard. Mr. Schultz had explained to all the children at the school how badly the Métis and Indians were being treated. The land had belonged to them in the first place, but the government had sent in surveyors to divide it up into new sections. And now the white farmers were trying to get property that had already been claimed by the Métis. Of course, they had complained to Ottawa, but the government had just ignored them. Nellie felt a real sympathy for them. She knew how she felt when Mother told her what to do, but she knew that some day she would grow up, and then she wouldn't be bossed around. What would happen to Louis Riel's followers, though? How unfair could Ottawa be? And how could her father and Mr. Ingram agree with the government on this one thing? They disagreed with them on almost everything else.

Nellie was shocked out of her thoughts by the sound of Hannah's quiet, firm voice. "They were here before us," she was saying. "And they should not be treated like this. There should not be this delay with their patents for land they've already claimed and worked. It should not be taken from them. There's more than enough for all of us. And *they* are willing to negotiate the matter."

Mr. Ingram set his jaw, and Mother stared at Hannah in shock. But Hannah continued: "It is not Louis Riel who is causing the trouble — it is the stupidity of the government in Ottawa, and if settlers are killed by the Indians, the government will be the guilty party. A few words of explanation, a few concessions, and peace would be restored."

"My God, girl, that's treason!" said Mr. Ingram. "Be careful how you repeat that outside your own home. In some countries today, you'd be shot for saying less."

Hannah was not ruffled by Mr. Ingram's comments. She just smiled and straightened her apron.

But Mr. Ingram's words still hung heavy in Nellie's ears. She felt she could not leave Hannah to face this alone. So she blurted out, "The government should — "

"That's quite enough, Nellie," Mother said.

"Let her say her piece, Mother," Will objected. "What harm can it do? And anyway it's Christmas day."

"Well, I don't like it, but since it's Christmas . . ."

Nellie gave Will a grateful glance. "The government should talk with the half-breeds," she said. "Instead they tell them to behave or they'll send out an army. They won't even listen." Nellie could hear Mr. Ingram clearing his throat. "In fact, they are making problems for them by taking their land and their buffalo. So what do they have to lose by fighting for what belongs to them? And how can anyone blame them?" Nellie did not wait for an answer. She ran from the room.

"It seems our schoolteacher, Mr. Schultz, has been filling the girls' heads with some strange ideas," Nellie heard Mr. Ingram say as she mounted the stairs to her room. "I shall speak to the school trustees about this matter."

"And I shall speak to Mr. Schultz," Mother said.

A few minutes later Nellie heard Hannah come into the bedroom. "Don't worry, Nellie," Hannah said as she came over to her sister, who was lying stretched out on the bed. "They're talking about something else now and have forgotten all about us."

"Do you think Mother will really go to school to see Mr. Schultz?" Nellie asked.

"She may, but I think it'll all be forgotten by the end

of the holidays. And I'm not going to ruin the next two weeks of my Christmas holidays worrying about it."

Nellie sighed. She wished she could be as practical as Hannah instead of being such a worrier.

****

Nellie sat by the kitchen window and looked out at the road. Hannah would soon be returning from her first day back at school, and Nellie wanted to know how things had gone. Mother was still angry, and Nellie had spent the entire Christmas holiday worrying that she would bustle down to the school one day and accuse Mr. Schultz of treason. She was so worried that she was barely able to eat or sleep. She had lost a lot of weight, too, and Mother was afraid she was coming down with galloping consumption. Nellie knew she didn't have consumption, but she was sick enough that Mother made her stay home from school. The only consolation in this was that Mother also had to stay home to take care of her. And that meant she could not get away to see Mr. Schultz.

"Nellie, you've got two glasses of milk to drink yet," Mother said. Mother was making her drink a quart a day to keep up her strength, and Nellie hated milk.

"Yes, Mother," she said as she sipped the lukewarm liquid. She scratched a little spot on the window clear of frost and could see two figures coming up the laneway to the house. The first one was Hannah, but she could not see who the second one was.

Then, as the figures drew closer, she thought the second one looked like Mr. Schultz. She could not believe her eyes. Hannah must have told him about Mother, and he must have come to confront her. She turned around to see if Mother had noticed. But she was peering into the oven, checking the pork roast she was cooking for supper.

Nellie flew to the door, grabbed her coat and hat, and was out the back door in a minute, heading for the barn. She could not face the scene that would follow. She ran up to the hayloft because she knew the men would be on the lower floor cleaning out the stables. Snuggled up in the hay, she tried to picture the scene in the house, but she could not bring herself to imagine what might be happening. Would Mother bring up the topic? Or would Mr. Schultz tell her what Hannah had said?

Nap came bounding through the barn door and over to Nellie. He was bigger than he had ever been and had grown a whole new coat of thick hair since his fight with the boar. Nellie burrowed her face and hands into the dog's fur. He was warm, and for a while she just sat and hugged him. But before long she realized that she would have to return to the house. It would not help matters if she really did catch cold. As she opened the kitchen door, she could hear the sound of a man's voice coming from inside.

"Mrs. Mooney, you are a very resourceful woman. Who would have thought a dollop of honey and some butter and vinegar would do my throat so much good? I'm sure I'll soon be on the road to recovery."

It was Mr. Schultz who was talking. He was huddled beside the stove in the big rocking chair with a quilt over his shoulders. Mother was stirring up pork gravy and smiling at the schoolteacher.

"Oh, Nellie, there you are. I came to see you. Hannah said you weren't well." He stopped to hold his sides while he coughed. "But your mother has kindly started to doctor *my* cold. I think she has her hands full with the two of us, don't you?"

"Yes," Nellie nodded. "But I'm not really sick. It's just that I don't feel like eating much."

"Well, you have to eat to keep up your strength, you know. And it must be easy to do that around here. I don't mind saying your mother is the best cook in the whole countryside."

Nellie shot a glance at her mother to see how she was reacting to all this. Had she accused Mr. Schultz of treason yet? Or was she going to fatten him up and then pronounce sentence?

"Have a cinnamon roll, Nellie," Mother said, without turning around. "It'll be good for you. And Mr. Schultz, if you are not feeling better tomorrow morning, I'll keep you in bed. Hannah can look after the school for you very well, and a day in bed will break your cold."

Nellie stared at her mother in disbelief. Maybe Mr. Schultz had already been accused of treason and forgiven. Whatever had happened, it certainly appeared that he was not going to lose his job because of Mother.

"Mr. Schultz, I think what you need now is to soak your feet in a nice pan of hot mustard water," Mother went on.

"Oh, thank you, Mrs. Mooney, but if I did that, you'd see what big holes I have in my socks. And my wife would kill me if she found out someone had seen them. I'm supposed to take them home on weekends to have them mended, but I always seem to forget."

"In that case," Mother said, "I'll just have to knit you a new pair. Now let me get the mustard water, and then I'll knit you some socks in no time."

"You're very kind, Mrs. Mooney," Mr. Schultz smiled. Then he turned to Nellie and asked, "Can you knit?"

"A little," Nellie said, looking into her lap and feeling

a little embarrassed about the poem she had read in the fall.

"Well, don't miss this great opportunity to learn from your mother. She's a fine seamstress and nurse. I don't think I've been this well cared for since I was a boy."

****

Father and Mr. Schultz were sitting at the kitchen table, in the evening light. Nellie was at the other end, doing some algebra problems. Three days had passed before Mr. Schultz's cold had gone away, but he was now well enough to go back to school the next day.

Father was talking now. "Do you think there'll be any more trouble in Saskatchewan over this Riel issue?" Nellie's heart stopped.

Mr. Schultz cleared his throat. "I'm afraid there will be. And I do hope it doesn't spread here. Vengeance can only bring vengeance, and it's a sorry sight. But it's the fault of the government . . ."

Nellie opened her eyes wide and looked at Mother, who was stirring up a pot of bedtime gruel. She didn't seem to be bothered by what Mr. Schultz was saying.

"The government has sent overbearing agents out to talk with the Métis, and that has messed everything up. Good manners could have saved the day, but the government agents don't have any."

Father shifted a bit uneasily in his chair, then leaned over towards Mr. Schultz. "You're right," he said in a low voice. "A soft answer turneth away wrath."

"Right you are," Mr. Schultz said at normal volume. "Strange isn't it, Mr. Mooney, that after more than eighteen hundred years of Christian teaching, there still is so little of real Christianity in the world. Governments still think a bullet is the best argument."

Father looked straight back at Mr. Schultz and said, "It will come, and you are helping by teaching the children what justice and kindness are. In one generation the world could be turned around if people would follow those two principles."

"Your gruel's ready, John. Do you want it now?" Mother asked.

"Yes, Lettie, and I can bet Mr. Schultz here would like some, too. My wife makes the finest porridge in Manitoba. Something to warm the marrow of your bones before you go to bed. And I think Nellie should have a bowl, too."

Nellie liked gruel, mostly because her father did, but that night, she thought it was food for a queen. Her fears had all melted away in the heat of Mother's cold remedies.

"Now that's real tasty," said Mr. Schultz. "I've always thought gruel would taste like 'diluted pincushions,' the way Dickens described it. But this is something different."

Nellie knew what made it special. It was the nutmeg. The smell of goodwill and neighbourliness. Almost as good as lilacs after a rain or wild rose leaves pressed in the pages of an old book.

Nellie went to school the next day feeling as contented as she ever had in her life.

12

"The Indians are coming!" Billy Day shouted as he stomped up the schoolhouse steps in his muddy boots. Every head turned to the doorway.

"Take your seat, Billy," Mr. Schultz said, without turning from the blackboard. "School is in session." It was the twenty-fourth of April, and Billy had been at home all morning, helping his father with the seeding. It had been an early spring.

The students moved restlessly in their seats, and Nellie could see the fear in their eyes. Only Hannah looked calm.

Mr. Schultz cleared his throat. "We have nothing to fear from the Sioux. They come every year on their way to Brandon to sell their handiwork. It is the Cree, from Saskatchewan, who are at war. And the Sioux are not even friends of the Cree."

"Dad says to go home and get your guns ready and shoot to kill," Billy blurted out.

"That is the worst thing you could do," said Mr. Schultz. "A massacre could happen if they come in peace and we attack them. Who wouldn't defend themselves if attacked? Before the Sioux reach us, they will pass by my home, where my wife is taking care of our two little sons. I am not afraid for them, because I know they will be safe." The faces of the children showed obvious signs of relief. "Now go home and tell your parents to buy their baskets and offer them a cup of tea, the way they always do in the spring. Remember, you are messengers of peace. Take your job seriously."

Nellie pulled on her knitted coat before she rushed out the door and bolted down the steps into the bright sunshine. The air was moist and fresh, the way it always was before the mayflowers came to life. A few violets had already crept out along the pathway leading to the school.

Before the children had left the school yard, Mr. Schultz walked out onto the steps and spoke again, "Remember this country belonged to the Indians once, and they see us as usurpers. We took their land and drove out their best friend, the buffalo. Use your imagination now, and think what you would feel like if you saw another race living on land that had been yours: another colour; other ways of living; feeling themselves superior."

Bob often walked to and from school with the Mooney sisters now, and Nellie didn't really mind. She had liked Bob ever since he helped her with Nap.

"Nell, I know how to tell if they're really coming." Bob put his head to the ground and listened. Then he jumped to his feet and yelled, "Gol! They're comin'. I can hear them!"

"Oh, come on, Bob, you don't know anything about things like that. You're the reading expert, not the trail-blazing type."

"You think so, do you?" Bob countered, scrambling to his feet. "Well, if that's what ya think, why don't you put your ear to the ground."

Nellie dropped down to her knees and put her left ear to the ground. She did think she heard thudding, rumbling noises, which could have been the sounds of carts coming from the direction of the Tiger Hills.

"Nellie L., what are you doing kneeling on the ground? We have to get home!" Hannah was looking at her strangely.

"Yes, I know!" Nellie said, scrambling to her feet. "I was just listening to find out how far away the traders are."

Nellie, Bob, and Hannah stepped out ahead of the others and ran like the wind, looking south towards the Tiger Hills from time to time. Would the long caravan of creaking carts come over those hills?

"This is exciting," said Nellie as they approached the Ingrams' lane. "We're going to stop a massacre! We're going to be heroes!"

"It's fun, isn't it?" Bob grinned at Nellie. "But I guess our team is breaking up. This is where I leave you. Good luck!"

Bob's clear blue eyes sparkled with excitement for a few seconds before he turned. Then, his shoulders straight, he walked briskly down the long lane. Nellie turned back to Hannah, who was already a few steps ahead of her.

"All right, heroine of the day," Hannah said. "Let's go and guard the fort. Mother is going to be surprised to see us home so early."

They were almost home when they noticed something in their yard — Indian ponies hitched to carts, and strange dogs.

Nap came running up from the creek and ran in circles around the girls, nipping at their heels.

"They're already here, Hannah. What should we do?" Nellie asked.

"We have no choice but to go on. We must tell Mother not to be afraid." Hannah just kept walking, and Nellie stumbled along blindly behind her.

Nellie forgot everything Mr. Schultz had said and began to think of all the massacre stories she had heard. Maybe the Sioux had killed Mother and Lizzie and were on their way out to the fields to kill the men. That would explain why everything was so quiet in the yard.

Hannah had almost reached the door ahead when Nellie was struck with a feeling of guilt for lagging behind, so she spurted ahead to catch up with her sister and went sprawling into the flowerbed beside the back door.

"Are you all right?" Hannah asked.

Nellie jumped up quickly. "Yes, I'm fine," she said, but she really wasn't. Her skirt had flown up, and she had scraped her knee against a stone. Her knee was all dirty and bloody, and it hurt terribly.

Hannah opened the kitchen door, and they stopped in their tracks. Mother was sitting in the rocking chair, surrounded by a group of Sioux women and their children. The smell of burned willow roots and tanned hide filled the air.

Hannah walked over to Mother while Nellie could only limp a few feet into the room. She leaned against the table, trying not to look as if she was in pain.

"Shut the door, girls, and look at this little baby," said Mother, taking a child from the arms of a woman in front of her. She hadn't noticed the pained look on Nellie's face. "He's been sick, poor baby, but I think he'll get better now. Mary Paul," she said, speaking to the mother, "wrap him up so his feet don't come out, and keep this flannel blanket on him. That'll do the wee fellow some good." Nellie recognized the mother now. She had come to the house last year to trade, and she and Nellie's mother had talked a lot about taking care of sick children then. Nellie was glad she was never going to have children. They seemed to be sick all the time.

"Whatever happened to you, child?" said a voice nearby.

Nellie jumped a bit, then winced in pain. The voice belonged to one of the older Sioux women, who had noticed Nellie limping.

"It's my knee. I fell on it just now." Nellie drew up her skirt to show the woman her scratched knee.

"Oh, a big scrape . . . Now you sit right down on that blanket while I get something for you. Nellie sat on the woman's bright blanket and waited. The woman shuffled slowly over to a leather bag sitting on the floor and brought out a withered, green, oval-shaped leaf. "Toad leaf," she said. She cleaned off the cut and wrapped the leaf firmly around Nellie's knee and tied it with a piece of an old towel.

"Thank you," Nellie said politely. She would act friendly, but she doubted this woman could possibly offer her any medicine as good as her mother's. Still she supposed the leaf wouldn't hurt.

"It'll draw out the soreness and heal. I'll show you where you can pick fresh leaves before I go. You have some at the edge of your yard."

Nellie felt a bit faint, so she stayed on the woman's blanket and looked around the kitchen. Just then

Lizzie came out of the pantry carrying a plate piled high with cheese and chicken sandwiches. Everyone took one or two, and they ate in silence.

"Now girls," said Mother, once everyone had had something to eat, "why don't you each pick out a straw basket for yourselves. They're beautifully woven."

"My ear hurts bad," one of the older women moaned. Mother poured a little water into a large china bowl and placed it on the table. Then she took a fresh cloth from a drawer, washed the woman's ear with a little soft soap, and put a few drops of laudanum in it. Then she took a roasted onion out of the warming oven on top of the stove, wrapped it in a piece of white broadcloth and gave it to the woman to hold over her ear. "It'll draw out the infection," she said.

"Now, try to walk on your leg a little." The older woman was leaning over Nellie. "You come over to the doorway. You'll see where you can get some more toad leaf." Nellie smiled. She would try. She stepped on her leg and to her surprise, the knee did feel a little better.

Nellie watched as the woman went over to the far side of the dooryard gate and stooped down to pick something. Then she brought it back to Nellie and put it in her hand.

"That's not toad leaf; that's plantain!" Nellie exclaimed.

"No, toad leaf," the woman smiled.

"Well, we call it plantain. It grows here every year, but we thought it was a weed."

"Many plants help us," said the woman. "I can tell your mother about uses for many more." She smiled at Nellie and then went back into the house. Nellie followed her to the kitchen, where the medicine woman showed Mother Nellie's knee.

Then Mother and the medicine woman began talking about the bursitis in Father's shoulders.

"You get sweet flag for that," said the older woman, "from the sloughs. They also call it muskrat root because muskrats like to eat it. You take the sweet flag and boil it with cedar boughs. Then bathe your husband's shoulders in this. It will make the pain less, and maybe heal him."

"Thank you," Mother said. "I shall do that."

As the Sioux women loaded their carts in the yard, Nellie went over to her mother and hugged her. "Oh, Mother, I was so scared. I thought you had been massacred."

"What would make you think such a thing, Lass? Mary Paul and all those other women . . . they come every year to sell. I've never known a bairn with such a wild imagination."

"But Billy Day . . ." Nellie said, letting her mother go and stepping back on her wounded leg.

"Oh, Nellie, you know Billy Day was just overexcited," said Hannah sensibly.

Someone knocked on the door. It was Mary Paul, carrying a grass mat with a pattern woven from porcupine quills.

"This is for you, Mrs. Mooney. I won't forget your kindness."

Mary Paul walked out and shut the door.

"Now, Nellie," said Mother, laughing. "Can you just imagine that lovely woman hacking us to bits! They're our neighbours — and fine ones, too."

Nellie walked over to the window. She could see the medicine woman climbing onto a sleek pony. Large saddlebags hung down over its flanks. Nellie wondered if the woman carried her medicines in them. If she was the doctor for her community, she probably knew a lot of different medicines. Nellie thought it strange that there were no white women doctors. At least, she had never heard of any. But why shouldn't there be women doctors?

The medicine woman was the last in line, and as she reached the road, she turned and looked back. From the window, Nellie waved, and the woman raised her arm to say goodbye before turning on down the road.

13

"Nellie, your cuff is trailing all over the cinnamon buns!" Lizzie reached across the table and lifted Nellie's sleeve out of the plate.

It was the winter of 1888, and the girls were at Will's new house, laying out food for a dance. Nellie was so short for her fourteen years she was worried she would never reach the five-foot mark. At least her hair was long, though. It was even long enough now to wear a fancy bow on the side.

Almost three years had passed since the Sioux raiders had visited the Mooneys' farm. That had been April 24, 1885, the day the guns roared at Fish Creek. Within three months the Northwest Rebellion had come to a tragic end, with the death sentence of Louis Riel. A wave of relief had swept through the English settlements in Western Canada. No one believed that Riel would actually be hanged, but this changed to disbelief when no reprieve came from Ottawa. The fiery defender of the Métis was hanged in November, and Mr. Schultz closed the school for a day of mourning.

These thoughts were far from Nellie's mind tonight, however. A few days ago Father had taught Nellie how to dance the Fisher's Hornpipe — out in the stable, while they were doing chores, far from Mother's eyes. Tonight was her big chance to show everyone how well she did it. "Strike into this one," Father had said. "Tap with your left and whirl on your right and you'll have them all watching you!"

"Nellie, now you've got your cuffs in the doughnuts," Lizzie giggled. She sounded like a girl again, but she wasn't anymore. In June of 1887, she had married Tom Rae, and they were now living in a new wooden house between the Mooneys and the Ingrams. She had come over to Will's this afternoon to help Mother and Nellie with the preparations.

"I guess I'm not watching what I'm doing . . . I'm so excited," said Nellie, grinning at Lizzie. Nellie knew she was expected to act more like a lady now that she was older. But somehow she had the feeling she would always have an impish streak, like her father. "I love this royal blue dress with the white cuffs, and look how it turns!"

Nellie started into the Fisher's Hornpipe, wishing Hannah, too, had been there to see her. But she would have to wait until Christmas for that. Hannah had gone to Winnipeg in September to study at the Normal School. No one was surprised that she had been accepted. She had had the highest marks at the Northfield School.

"Well done, Sparrowshins," Nellie imagined her father saying as she finished the dance with a full twirl, which she added for effect.

"Careful, Nellie L., I can see your petticoat! You'd better not do that one at the dance!" Lizzie said with a little smile. Dear Lizzie was a bit tired these days because she was expecting her first child, but she was as kind as ever. Nellie grinned back at her sister.

"Maybe I can dance at Will's wedding, too!" she said gleefully — for Will was to be married soon to a thin, graceful girl named Lily. She was in the kitchen helping Mother prepare coffee.

"We'll be having a good time tonight," Will said, coming over to the table and admiring the spread. It's crowded in here, but I've been at plenty of dances where we didn't have nearly as much room. Good thing to have the dance now — before the partitions go up."

****

Evening came at last, with moonlight streaming over the snow and the sky full of stars. Nellie and Mrs. Ingram and Lizzie had begun setting out the lemonade and coffee and cutting jelly cakes, cinnamon buns, and apple and strawberry pie. Then, at about seven o'clock, they could hear sleighbells, as the neighbours came towards the house in their cutters.

"Whoo, it's a bitter wind out there," Bert Ingram said as he came puffing through the door, shaking the snow off his bearskin coat. "I've got double blankets on the horses tonight."

"Hey, Jack," Billy Day shouted as he stumbled in out of the cold, "leave some of those doughnuts for me."

Jack was standing at the end of the food table, sneaking cookies and squares.

"Have a coffee, Billy," Jack shot back with unusual good humour. "There's lots and the ladies are serving." At breakfast that morning, Jack had said he didn't like dancing, so Nellie wasn't sure why he was in such a good mood. Then she noticed something new. Abigail Adams appeared in the doorway with a black fur hat and muff that made her look like a queen. She scanned the room anxiously, but when she spotted Jack, she smiled and brushed back her golden hair. A smile crept across Jack's face. Then he blushed and scooped a couple of doughnuts off the table.

Nellie tried to stop staring. So maybe Jack will change his mind one day about living alone all his life. But Abigail Adams? She and Abigail had almost become friends. They had had fun competing against each other for top place in their class. But would Abigail never stop acting so superior? The way she brushed back her hair reminded Nellie of her first day at school when Abigail had strutted up to the front in her gleaming braids and fancy outfit.

More guests came tumbling in to the sound of sleighbells and laughter until the room was packed to the rafters.

"Welcome, ladies and gentlemen," the caller shouted above the chatter. "Let's begin."

"Come on, Nell, let's go." It was Bob Ingram. Nellie was not one to turn down a dance, so she happily glided onto the floor with him. Even though he was still thirteen, Bob was taller than Nellie, taller even than Hannah, and a fair dancer. Not as good as Nellie, of course — but then he had not had dancing lessons.

They were just finishing the first dance when the fiddlers started in on the "Fisher's Hornpipe" and Nellie got her chance. "Dance to your partner, and corner the same," said the caller. Nellie sailed around the centre of the room in a fine twirl with her hands on her hips.

As she turned and tapped her feet in perfect time to the music, she did not notice that all the other dancers had fallen back to watch the performance. But then she heard clapping and realized that she was dancing alone in the centre of the floor. When she saw her father's smiling face and heard the loud cheers around her, she tapped on her left and whirled on her right, stopping only when the music ended.

"Hurray for Nell," Bob said as everyone clapped.

Just then, Mother appeared out of nowhere and grabbed her by the arm. "You should not be making such a show of yourself. Why, you've been showing off your legs like some play-acting woman. Go right upstairs and quiet down." She gave Nellie a little nudge with her arm. "And you can stay there until the refreshments are served. You'll find three babies on the bed that you can take care of. Their mothers are all busy down here. Now go on, this minute."

Nellie felt her face turning deep red. Bob stood beside her, shuffling uncomfortably. As Mother went to step between them, Nellie turned and ran for the stairs, stumbling into Jack and Abigail as she went. "Serves you right, Nellie," Jack scowled, but Abigail gave her a sympathetic nod.

Nellie rushed for the open stairway but was stopped by a pat on her shoulder. It was Father. "Well, done, Sparrowshins," he said, smiling quietly. Nellie stopped and grinned, and then with her head held high, walked the rest of the way to the room above.

When Nellie reached the top of the stairs, she could hear the music starting up again. All the dancers would be falling into line, and here she was, stuck in the attic. How could Mother do this to her! She stormed across the hall and over to the bedroom where the babies were sleeping.

There were three of them lying on the bed. One had a sour smell of stale food on his clothes and cried out at times in his sleep. The second one was small and pale-faced. She was sleeping quietly in her pink blanket. The third one squirmed about as she slept and had already worked her way down to the other end of the bed. Since they were all sleeping, Nellie slumped into a rocking chair, hoping they wouldn't waken. She didn't want babies spitting up all over her party dress.

What a lot of work babies are, Nellie thought as she dropped off to sleep. Their mothers always looked tired. Poor Mrs. Dale. She looked paler every time Nellie saw her. "Well, I'll never get married," Nellie thought, "so I won't have babies to worry about. Babies are all right for older women who don't like sports and dances, but not for me."

****

"Wake up!"

Nellie opened her eyes and saw Liz standing beside the rocking chair, nudging her shoulder. "Mother didn't mean you to stay up here all this time. It's nearly dawn and everyone's leaving!"

Nellie opened her eyes wider, then jumped up from the chair. "No more dancing? Why didn't Mother come and get me if she didn't want me to stay here so long? It's not fair!"

"Tom is going to take you and me home now. Mother said the rest of the cleanup can wait till later in the morning. Everyone is just too tired now! But it was a lovely party!"

"And I missed the whole thing! Oh, Lizzie! How could Mother do this to me? How could she! Just because I danced one dance alone. And no one else thought it was terrible — even Father clapped."

"I don't know, Nellie, but hurry now. It's all over."

Nellie stumbled down the stairs behind Lizzie in a state of fury. She'd only had one dance with Bob, and Bob's older brother, Bert, had asked her to save him a dance, too. Then there was Jimmy Sloan, the boy from the next farm. He was almost twenty years old, and yet he'd asked her to be sure to save him a dance. She could hardly believe everything was over and she'd missed out on the fun. It would be ages again before there was another party this grand. Houses didn't get built that often. She stamped past Mother without a word, grabbed her coat, boots, and muff, and tromped out the door.

In the sleigh, Nellie shivered at the sight of the grey, icy dawn sky, but smiled a frozen smile when she saw a welcoming column of smoke coming out of the Mooneys' chimney. It was a terrible thing to have missed most of the party just because of one dance, Nellie thought. But maybe it was worth it. There was nothing quite like doing a Hornpipe for a whole crowd of people, dancing and twirling and not caring a fig about anything else. Nellie snuggled under the buffalo robe. At least some people appreciated her, and some day when she was grown up, she would go to other parties and dance all night. Mother wouldn't be able to spoil her fun forever.

14

"I could use a couple of nice steamy muffins right this minute," Nellie said to herself as she crunched through the snow on her way home from school. It was February and so cold, her boots squeaked as they hit the ground.

Now that Lizzie was living next door, Nellie dropped in for coffee every day after school. She would sit laughing and petting Lizzie's big orange cat, Peter, and telling Lizzie all about her plans for the future. Since the party at Will's, she had decided she would dance only for fun and not as a professional, so now she had to think of something else to do. And there were not many jobs available to women. She knew she did not want to be a farmer's wife. But she might make a good teacher. Then she would have her own income and be independent — and a teacher was always greatly respected in the community. She would have the opportunity to teach girls how to read so they would not be ignorant and let their husbands treat them badly. As a teacher she would be able to help women.

Lizzie would listen to Nellie's schemes but would never sit still for long. She was always working at something. Her kitchen had the best-scrubbed floor in the Millford region, and the rest of the house was just as spotless. Even though her baby was due in two months, she did her share of the barn work, too. She milked the cows when Tom was busy cutting wood and doing other outside chores, and she gathered the eggs and fed the hens every day.

"Hello . . . anybody home?" Nellie called out as she stepped into the back entrance to the kitchen.

The unwashed breakfast dishes still sat on the cupboard by the sink. A half-loaf of bread and an open crock of butter lay beside them. Nellie looked over to the couch to see if Lizzie was resting, but she was not there. Even the rocking chair, the cat's favourite spot, was empty. By this time of the day Lizzie was usually hurrying around, preparing the evening meal. But she was nowhere in sight.

"Lizzie . . ." Nellie called again.

No one answered. Then she heard the sound of a baby's cry. She rushed through the doorway and headed for the stairs but stopped in her tracks when she saw, not Lizzie, but her mother coming towards her.

"Mother! Why are you here?" Nellie burst out. Then she saw the strained look on her mother's face. "What is it, Mother? Did something happen?"

Mother looked over her shoulder, put her finger to her lips, and steered Nellie back to the kitchen. Then she wiped her hands on her apron and cleared her throat. "It's . . . it's Lizzie, dear . . . and her baby . . . The baby came too soon." Mother took a deep breath and went on. "Lizzie was gathering eggs in the henhouse and slipped on a loose board. She . . . she managed to get back to the house and pull the pole bell." Mother moved a chair out from the kitchen table and sat down. "Thank goodness Tom heard the bell and came running; then he called me and went for the doctor. But there was nothing even the doctor could do."

"But I heard . . . a baby," Nellie said.

"Yes, we'll do our best, but the doctor thinks it doesn't have a chance. It's a boy, though, a little boy."

"And Lizzie?" Nellie asked, biting her lower lip to keep from crying.

"Your sister is going to make it. But for a while, we weren't sure." Mother got up and walked over to the stove. There was a little cradle between it and the far wall that Nellie had not noticed till now.

"We're keeping it as warm as we can for the baby," Mother said. He was rolled in many folds of flannel, and Nellie could see only his sweet little wrinkled face. His eyes were tightly closed, but his tiny mouth opened like a bird's. He made a sad little squeak that cut right through Nellie's heart.

"We'll do the very best we can for him," Mother said. "Now, run home and bring me a little milk, and we'll try to feed him with an eye dropper. He's too weak to suck, and Lizzie doesn't have any milk yet."

****

Nellie was leaning over the little baby in the cradle, trying to feed him from a bottle that Mother had prepared. She had been helping care for Lizzie and the baby for two days now; there was no more time for books and school. Her only goal in life was to get the little one to drink some milk — but so far, he had taken none. Nellie sighed and felt very alone. Mother was sleeping in the spare room and Tom was resting on the front room couch, so Nellie was the only one keeping vigil. She could not be angry at them for sleeping, though. They had not slept since the baby's birth.

The kitchen was dark except for the pool of light from the coal-oil lamp on the table. The baby whimpered, and Nellie picked up the small bundle. To her surprise, he stopped crying as soon as she began to walk him back and forth across the room. As Nellie looked down at the little triangular face, she tightened her arms around him. His tiny mouth opened and seemed to draw in air in small gasps. Maybe she had been wrong about babies. Perhaps one day she would have one of her own after all. And maybe, just maybe, Lizzie's baby would live.

All week Mother and Nellie tried to feed him, but nothing worked. Even sugar wrapped in a cloth and put it in the baby's mouth to dissolve did not seem to make him stronger. And in the afternoon of the fifth day, he began to weaken noticeably as though he was too tired to breathe. He took in air now in sharp little gasps that seemed to draw in his tiny frame and tire him even more. Mother and Nellie were exhausted, but still they kept walking him back and forth, from one end of the kitchen to the other, keeping him as warm as possible, taking turns trying to feed him. Lizzie, weak from loss of blood, lay still on her bed, staring at the wall, and listening to her baby's low whimper.

The eerie quiet was broken by a knock on the kitchen door. "I've come to help," said Mrs. Ingram, stepping inside. Her blonde hair shone in the afternoon sun, and her kind smile warmed Nellie's heart.

"How is Lizzie?" Mrs. Ingram asked as she hung her coat on the peg beside the door.

"She's coming along slowly," Mother said. She was standing by the stove now, holding the baby. "She's past any danger, though."

Mrs. Ingram did not ask about the baby. She had dropped in briefly a couple of times before and knew he was doing poorly.

"The baby's growing weaker," Mother sighed. Then she turned to Nellie, "Why don't you go outside for a bit of air, dear. It's a sunny day, and Mrs. Ingram can help me now."

Nellie grabbed her coat and rushed out the door. She ran across the snowy yard to a knoll beyond it. If she had to listen to the baby's painful cries for one more minute, she would die, too. As the cold wind whipped across her face and stirred up the snow in front of her, she shivered a little and started to pray, "Please, please, God, make Lizzie's baby better. Please, God, if only you will, I'll walk him night and day until Lizzie's well and strong. Please, God." The tears were streaming down her face now. "You do hear him crying, don't you, God?" She stood there sobbing. The wind just whistled by. God did not seem to be answering her.

Exhausted finally, she wiped her face with her hands and turned back to the house. She could not stay away any longer. If the baby was crying again, she would walk him. It always helped when she did that. He turned his little face towards her and was quiet. She could do *that* for him if nothing else. She hurried back to the house, wishing she had not stayed outside so long.

Inside, the kitchen was silent. Mother and Mrs. Ingram were standing with their backs to the door, staring down at the cradle. Nellie asked no questions. She knew that the little baby had gone from them.

****

They buried him in a small white coffin in the Millford cemetery that Saturday. Lizzie was still too sick to go, but Father and Mother and Jack and Nellie were there along with Tom and his parents. Mrs. Ingram had come over to stay with Lizzie for the afternoon.

Nellie went back to school the following Monday, not as sure of herself as she used to be. She could not forget the baby's tiny face and mouth, and she could still feel him turning his little head towards her chest. She realized now that someday she might marry and have children after all. Yet she knew that marriage was such a final thing, and for farm women, it was the end of all hopes and ambitions.

Farm women never had time for anything but work. Even Lizzie, who seemed to be so happy, was always busy scrubbing and cleaning, and doing chores around the barn, too. It was the only way the farm could keep running. And when Lizzie had children to care for, it would be that much harder. But her lot in life was much easier than poor Mrs. Dale's.

There were many women who had little hope of happiness, and none at all of getting an education. Their husbands expected them to work day and night, and most of them had a new baby every year. Nellie had no idea how they ever managed to keep up their spirits. Babies were so much work it was hard to imagine why anyone would have one, and yet there was Lizzie's baby, that poor sweet child.

Maybe, Nellie thought, maybe some day it would be better to have a baby than to have all the books and learning in the world.

Part Three

Nellie's Vision

15

Nellie tossed and turned in the heat of the July night. She was used to warm weather in the country, but that was nothing compared to the city. Here in Brandon the air was sticky and dusty and reeked of perspiration and horse manure.

It was over a year since Lizzie's baby had died, and poor Lizzie was finally starting to look happier. Nellie had finished her last term at Northfield School and now she was in Brandon, writing the exams that would let her into teacher's college. It was strange how things turned out sometimes. She had come with the two people she had hated most on her first day of school at Northfield — Bob Ingram and Abigail Adams.

Bob's family had always expected him to become a teacher or a minister. He had been such a good reader as a boy and he was still an excellent pupil. But lately he had become interested in breeding horses and had barely made the grade on the English exam at Northfield. He had been doing a horse trade the day before and had not had much time to study.

Bob had driven her and Abigail to Brandon in his buggy two days before. Then they had parted to look for lodging. Nellie had made a new green gingham dress for the occasion, and Abigail was wearing a pure white blouse and black and white striped skirt. They had felt like real grown ladies.

But as the afternoon wore on, they had become hotter and more and more impatient. Most rooms were far too expensive. They had finally settled for a steamy room in the attic of a run-down house right on the main street, but the landlady had given them no reduction for sharing.

So Nellie was now lying on a lumpy bed, hot and restless, thinking about her algebra exam the next day. She had never been very good at algebra but had always made it through because Hannah had helped her study. But Hannah wasn't here this time. She had found a job at Indian Head, west of Brandon, and had begun teaching there last September.

Nellie had already sailed through the literature and history exams, but algebra was different. Numbers just swam before her eyes when she tried to work out her equations. There was only one explanation: algebra must be a form of punishment for all the things she'd done wrong in her life.

"I can't stand it," she finally announced to Abigail, who was trying to sleep in the bed next to hers.

"Me neither," Abigail sighed. "And I don't know how we got stuck in this attic room. It's twice as hot here as anywhere else!"

"Yes, it's like an oven . . . Anyway, I can't sleep, so I

might as well sit by the window and try to get a bit of air."

Abigail turned over and faced the wall. In spite of Nellie's earlier resentment, she felt her heart go out to her roommate. The romance between Abigail and Jack had ended a few weeks before. They had liked each other, but Abigail had no intention of becoming a farm wife, and farming was the only thing Jack had ever wanted to do.

Nellie walked to the window in her white cotton nightdress and gazed out at the street below. She had really tried to study, but nothing seemed to stay in her head. So the only thing to do now was resign herself to failing. She held her head up and determined to go to her fate gracefully — like Anne Boleyn or Mary, Queen of Scots. The thought consoled her for a few minutes. Then panic set in again. Without a pass in algebra, she would not get her entrance papers for Normal School. She sank to her knees and, with her hands on the windowsill, prayed for God to help her.

She was only a few words into her prayer when she heard a Salvation Army band coming down the street. Above the sound of the fife and drum came a thin, clear woman's voice, singing:

> Do not fear the gathering clouds of sorrow,
> Tell it to Jesus, tell it to Jesus,
> Are you anxious what will be tomorrow,
> Tell it to Jesus alone.

As the band played and the words rang out, Nellie felt a shaft of comfort come into her heart. She had wrestled with that old algebra and maybe she had lost, but she had done her best. If now was the hour of her thwarted dreams, let it be so.

****

The next day Nellie and Abigail walked to the examination hall in silence. The paper was long and full of words Nellie had never seen before. She heard deep sighs all around her and let out quite a number herself. Then she remembered the advice Mr. Schultz had given her. "Remember, Nellie," he had said, "every second counts in an exam. So do not waste time worrying about what you don't know. Just work first on the problems you can solve best."

She worked slowly through three questions, then looked up at the clock. It was already 11:15. Only forty-five minutes left to try three more.

She plunged in and finished the next question in fifteen minutes. Some students were beginning to hand in their papers. Abigail strutted confidently past her desk, followed by Bob, who stumbled along with his head down. That Abigail, Nellie thought. Some things about her will never change. Nellie pushed the thought out of her head and kept writing. No one would be able to say she hadn't kept trying until the very last minute.

All too soon, however, the presiding officer banged his desk with a ruler to mark the end of the exam. "All papers in now," he ordered, peering over his glasses. "That means everyone," he said, looking straight at Nellie.

Out in the sunshine the steps to the exam hall were blocked by a cluster of chattering students.

"What did you get for question three?" a boy with thick wire-rimmed glasses was asking a girl with blonde hair tied in a knot at the back of her head.

Nellie spotted Bob and touched his arm. "I don't want to hear this," she said. "I don't want to know I failed. Let's go before they start asking us questions."

"Yeah, I'm tired of all this, too. It's bad enough writing the exam. You don't have to make things worse by talking about it after. Let's go for a ride in my buggy. Maybe that'll help us forget." Bob looked over at her and grinned the way he had the time she'd directed him to go through the muddy barnyard.

They walked down the main street to the livery stable and took the buggy out. Bob guided his chestnut mare through the lunchtime crowds and headed towards the open fields around Brandon.

Nellie stared straight ahead and said nothing.

"Don't worry about it so much, Nellie," Bob said. "There's a lot more to life than just passing exams."

Nellie looked at Bob sitting there beside her. He had grown into a handsome fellow, and most girls would have loved to go for a ride in the country with him. Nellie had to admit that she didn't mind either.

It was cooler outside town, and tiger lilies grew in thick bunches beside the roadway. The scent of freshly mown hay drifted across the fields. Nellie started to relax a little.

"Bob, if I fail that algebra paper, my whole world will fall apart. All my plans and dreams burned up in just three hours. And I don't know what I'll do if I can't teach."

"Well, first of all, Nellie you probably didn't fail. I've noticed that the ones who come out bragging often don't know enough to know what they don't know. You probably did better than you think."

"Yes, I may have passed, but just barely. How do you think you did, Bob?"

"Oh, I'm not at all sure . . . Not so well, but I don't

mind if I don't go to Normal School. If I failed, I'll stay home and keep raising Clydesdales . . . especially now that Bert has his own farm. Pa wouldn't mind if I stayed on and helped with the horses. And you know, Nellie, I love the work."

"Yes, you could have a good future there, raising choice horses. I can see you doing that and being happy. And you'll marry and probably be chairman of the local school board and the summer fair committee."

"Well if I do, I'll let girls enter races — and win them, too!"

Nellie smiled. "I know you will. And you'll have a good life with your Clydesdales and your family. But don't forget to give readings at the local fairs!"

"Readings? Never! Remember how Mother used to drag me all over the country to read to her friends?" Bob shivered. "How embarrassing! But I'll probably run for the school board and give speeches."

"But if *I* fail," Nellie went on, "it'll be the end of me . . . of all my ambitions. I want to help people, especially poor farm women. I want to tell the world about their hardships and long days of heavy work. I want to write about the drudgery of their lives and the drastic economies they have to practise. No one can even read for long after dark, for coal oil is expensive. And shoeblack? Who can afford that? City folks, not us. We have to use lard and lamp soot. And the hours women have to work to keep up their households! I'll tell everyone how they help in the fields until there are enough sons to help with the outside work — that is if there *are* any sons. Then how after a heavy day they go right on preparing food and sewing while their husbands sleep. I'll be a voice for the voiceless like Charles Dickens, and I'll never marry!"

Nellie had forgotten Bob was there as she made her speech. She could see herself standing before a crowded theatre, telling the premier of Manitoba in a low ringing voice about the hardships suffered by women on the farms of Manitoba. "No one's ridicule will ever stop me, for I know I am right. And no matter what they say, I will keep on. Did you know, Bob, that women do *not* have the vote?"

Bob chuckled. "How can I not know that, with you around?"

"Yes, I guess I have mentioned it before."

The sun was shining across Nellie's face and she was smiling now.

"But, Bob, don't you see? When women have the vote, then conditions will improve. The law will protect women instead of taking away all their property and belongings when they marry. And they'll be called persons by the court. Did you know that a woman is not even considered a person according to Canadian law?"

"No, I didn't know that . . . but what does that have to do with you?"

"Well, things don't change by just wishing. If I could teach people by my writing and giving lectures, I could help change the laws. The way Dickens did for the poor, through his writing. It's all I really care about. But if I fail algebra, all my hopes and dreams will be dashed to the ground." Nellie's eyes began to fill with tears.

"Well, if you fail, you could get married," Bob said, smiling. "You could be a wife, like most other women."

"No, that would be terrible. You know I'm hopeless at housework. And I'm all thumbs when I try to knit or sew. Besides, a farmer's wife has no time to write!"

"If a man loved you, Nellie, he wouldn't care how good a housekeeper you were," Bob said firmly, "and he'd help so you'd have time to write!" The reins had grown slack now, and the horses had stopped to graze at the side of the road.

"No, Bob, if I married a farmer, I'd never have the chance to be anything else. You know how busy all the wives are."

"Well, then, maybe you could marry a teacher! I might still go to teacher's college if I pass all my exams!"

"No, Bob, that would be just as bad. Look at Mr. Schultz. His wages are so low he has to have a farm, too! And who runs it? His wife!"

"I didn't really want to be a teacher anyway," Bob mumbled.

"What did you say?"

"I don't think any man who loved you would mind that you couldn't cook or keep house, Nellie. At least life would never be boring. Remember the time you told everyone you saw a green wolf across the creek?"

"And you were the only one who believed me. Oh, Bob, I'm sorry about that tale I made up."

"Well, what I'm trying to say, Nellie, is that if you don't pass algebra, you might like to marry someone . . . someone like me, perhaps."

"Marry *you!* . . . Oh, you wouldn't want me." Nellie was almost speechless. She had never thought of Bob in this way. She liked him, and he had always been kind to her, even when she had been mean. But she could never be in love with him, and she would have to tell him.

"Bob, any woman would have to be out of her mind not to see what a fine husband you would make. But you . . . you wouldn't want me. I couldn't stay on the farm. You'll have a good life with your horses and you'll find a good wife. I know you will, and you'll be happy, but I just don't know what I'll do, Bob. I must pass this exam or . . ."

16

"Maybe it will be a good thing if you do fail," Mother was saying. "If you stayed home a bit longer, you might grow up a bit. It would do you no harm to have the conceit taken out of you."

"Do you really think I'm conceited?" Nellie protested.

Mother paused as she shaped loaves for the oven. "No, perhaps not, but you talk too much for a young girl. Anyway, the world will smooth you down."

It was almost the last week of August, and Nellie had spent the summer worrying about her exam results. If she'd passed, she could go on to a glorious life at Normal School. If she'd failed, she would have to return to the local school for the winter, then try the exams again next year. And that would mean staying at home with Mother for another twelve months. Nellie was almost a grown woman now, and

Mother still talked to her as if she were a child. Nelli respected her for her loyalty and good managemer but would never understand why she was so severe. Ne lie resolved never to be so harsh with her own chi dren — if she ever had any.

"I really am afraid I failed the algebra, Mother."

"You'll do just fine, Nellie," said Hannah, walkin into the kitchen with a basketful of potatoes. She ha been home for the summer but would be going back t her pupils at Indian Head in September. "And you'll b a good teacher, Nellie."

Nellie looked at Hannah thoughtfully. "Yes, I think could be . . . if I just . . ."

"You've never failed an exam in your life, and I can' think you will now," Mother said, somewhat im patiently.

"Yes, Nellie, just try not to think about the algebra Have Bob or Abigail received their results yet?"

"No . . . but . . . Bob has his horses, and . . . Abigail is confident she passed."

"Well, you'll soon be notified of the results, and I bet you'll have higher marks than either Abigail or Bob."

"But not as high as yours," Nellie answered and she was probably right. Hannah had passed with the highest marks in the province when she had tried the entrance exams two years before.

****

The fatal day was drawing near. It was the second last Saturday in August, and Nellie was driving the buggy into Millford to pick up the mail and supplies. She had volunteered for the job because she knew the exam results would be in and she wanted no one else to see them before she did. Jack had objected at first because he loved riding into town. But in the end the family had let her go.

As the grey mare clopped along, Nellie looked across the fields and thought of all the hard labour that was done on farms. There was the harvest and the never-ending cycle of taking cattle to pasture, milking them, and turning them back to pasture. And there were other chores, too — like the fight against weeds. She would get the garden clear only to look out two weeks later and find the things sprouting up all over again. It was so hard and useless and boring. And the money was terrible. If the farmers were lucky, there would be just enough to pay expenses when the grain was sold in the fall. Father didn't even expect to clear enough to send her to the Normal School. The crops had been better two years ago when Hannah had gone. Thank goodness Hannah had offered to pay Nellie's expenses. With her savings and a big part of her teacher's wages, Nellie would have just enough.

Nellie's heart was in her throat as she pulled up to the Millford post office and walked in the door.

"No mail for you folks today," the postmaster said when he saw Nellie. "Nothing except this." He pulled a card from the Mooneys' mail slot and pushed it across the counter.

Nellie could have cried as she took it from him and headed for the door. "Miss Nellie L. Mooney," the card said. With shaking hands, she turned it over and tried to read the words on the other side. "Having passed the recent Second Class Teacher's Examination, you are eligible to attend the September-to-February session of the Normal School at Winnipeg." Nellie's heart was suddenly filled with overwhelming relief, and she threw the card into the air.

"Good news?" the postmaster asked.

"The best of my life! I've been accepted at Normal School!" Nellie grinned at the postmaster, picked the card off the floor, and then stepped lightly out the door.

The road home might as well have been paved with gold. And the sun shone down like an old friend. Nellie had passed the first hurdle and nothing could stop her now. She was no longer a prisoner of the farm.

She would not have to stay another year and do whatever Mother asked. She would not have to lock horns with Jack. And Father and Hannah and Lizzie and Will would be so proud of her. Even Mother and Jack would be — in their own way. As she turned the mare into the laneway, she noticed Jack standing by the gate.

"Where the devil have you put the monkey wrench?" he shouted before she'd even stepped out of the buggy.

"The monkey wrench?"

"Yes, you were the last one to use it, and we can't find it anywhere. We've been held up fixing the binder. The whole afternoon's been wasted!" Nellie stared back at him blankly. She could remember using it to turn a bolt on the buggy before she left, but she could not remember where she had put it after that. Then she looked down and, to her horror, saw the missing wrench lying on the floor.

She reached down silently and gave it to Jack. There was nothing to say. Jack took the wrench, gave her a look of disgust, and stamped off to the field.

Nellie got down from the buggy, stuffed the postcard in her pocket, and headed for the barn. She would do the milking instead of having supper. Nobody would care if she didn't show up at the table. Jack sure wasn't interested in her results. It was obvious that the monkey wrench was more important than she was, but someday she'd prove she wasn't useless at everything.

And when she became a teacher, she'd mail the family a whole box of monkey wrenches — paid for out of her own salary.

****

Nellie came out of the barn with the last of the milk just as twilight was beginning to fall, and stopped in her tracks. Jack was sitting on a log outside the doors. "You didn't need to do the milking all alone, Nellie. You knew I'd be down to help as soon as supper was over," he said quietly.

Nellie nodded but said nothing.

"I'm sorry about yelling at you when you came home," he went on, "but you know how rushed we are just now with the harvest and all. We're trying to get the crop in before the rain comes and ruins it."

Nellie stood in the half-light, looking at the ground. Jack was trying to do his job and he was doing it bravely even though his heart was broken.

"Say, kid, what's the matter?" Jack asked. "Did you fail? Everybody thinks so. We were all talking about it at supper. Mother thought we should just let you be for a while."

Nellie said nothing. She thought she might as well keep him guessing.

"Don't take it so hard, Nellie," Jack said. "You're young, and you already have a good education. No one can take that away from you. . . . You're better off than I am. . . . I was always too ready to work and pretend I didn't care about going to school. I said I wanted to be a man and drive horses and haul out the grain. But I really did care . . . at least I do now, though I've been a big fool in some ways."

Nellie could not believe what she was hearing. She

sat down beside Jack. All her bitter feelings towards him were melting away. "Jack, I'm sorry about the monkey wrench," she said. "And you're only twenty. You could still go back to school and learn and you'd do fine. I know you would."

"No, it's too late now. Besides, I want to farm."

"And . . . and . . . I didn't fail," Nellie smiled. "I passed . . . even the algebra!"

Jack grinned at Nellie and said, "I'm glad for you, Nellie. Really I am!"

"Do you mean it?"

"Of course, I do."

"Well, Jack, there isn't a boy in this whole countryside as good-looking as you, and you're the best farmer, too. I'm sorry I've been so lippy with you all the time," Nellie said. "It's just that I always thought you were picking on me. But you know something, I think we'll get on better now, even if we are both as stubborn as oxen."

"Yeah, I think we will . . . Now, let's get that milk into the milkhouse."

17

"Nellie L. Mooney, you're not going anywhere with your right shoe unbuttoned like that," Mother said.

Nellie looked down at her foot, and sure enough, the tongue of her new goatskin boot was flapping around. It was five in the morning, and she'd been up since four, getting ready to leave for Winnipeg.

"Here, let me button it up for you. No daughter of mine is going to show up in the city looking like a waif. Here, put your foot up on the stool." Mother leaned over and did up the neglected buttons.

"Now remember, Nellie, you are going to Normal School to learn. So hush your talk and listen to your elders. And don't go taking up with strangers. A girl can't be too careful these days."

"Better hurry up, Nell," Jack said, poking his head through the kitchen doorway. "You don't want to miss your train."

Nellie was sorry to be leaving Jack now that they were finally friends, but there was nothing to be done about it. She looked forward to her future bravely. It helped that she had a new dress to fortify her nerves — a green one, with brass buttons and black military braid, and underneath it, a blue and yellow crocheted petticoat.

"I'm all ready, Jack. But let me just go and say good-bye to Father."

Nellie took her new winter coat off the peg beside the door and walked out into the crisp September morning. A greyish-pink light was growing just above the horizon.

"Father, Father, I'm leaving," Nellie shouted into the barn. "Where are you?"

"Right here, Sparrowshins." Father came out from the cow stalls carrying a pail of milk. A few pieces of straw were sticking out of his green wool barn coat.

Nellie felt tears coming to her eyes.

"There, there, now, my girl. It's not so bad. You're going on an adventure and you'll be back at Christmas."

"I know . . . but . . ." Nellie let a tear fall down her cheek.

Father smiled. "Now let's get you packed into the buggy so your adventure can begin!"

Nap whizzed past Nellie, nearly knocking her off her feet. Now he was standing on the buggy floor with his tongue hanging out, looking at everyone.

"Oh, dear, sweet Nap, I wish you could come with me, but you'd hate it in Winnipeg."

Nap blinked both eyes as if to say he wouldn't mind Winnipeg one bit.

"Down, boy," Father said, "and make way."

Nellie lifted her skirt and jumped up into the buggy seat.

"Well, dear, safe journey," Father said. "You'll be much in our minds."

Mother just waved and touched her eye with the hem of her apron.

At the end of the lane, Nellie turned around to look back at the farm. She knew she would miss it, now that she was leaving. She could see Father going towards the house carrying a pail of fresh milk for breakfast, just as he always did, with Nap at his heels. And although she could not see her, Nellie knew that Mother would be back in the kitchen, stirring the porridge, just the way she did every morning.

****

At the Glenboro station, Jack unloaded Nellie's trunk and waited with her on the platform until the locomotive chugged into the station a few minutes later. To Nellie's surprise, there were more pigs and cows than passengers on the train.

"Must be the right train, Nellie. Looks like they've put on a special car for you and the pigs."

Nellie walked up the few steps into the train, then she made her way along the aisle and stopped at a seat by the window. She pushed her bag onto the rack above her head and waved out the window one last time, but Jack was walking back to the buggy and did not see her.

As the train rolled out of the station, Nellie looked out at the wheatfields shining gold in the early morning sun. She thought about the farmers who were always so busy working the land that they had no time to enjoy its beauty. She thought about Mrs. Dale and how old she always looked, tired out from working in the fields and barn and raising five children. Someday, she vowed, she would do something to free the women of the farms from their difficult lives.

The train chugged along on to the north, and Nellie settled back in her seat. "But first," she thought, "I'll have to buy a box of monkey wrenches!"

18

"There's no station at Somerset," the conductor said as he watched Nellie open her alligator purse and unpin the ticket stub for her trunk. "Are you sure someone's coming to meet you?"

"Oh, yes," Nellie said. "I'm the new teacher for the Hazel school. A trustee will meet me here and drive the last seventeen miles to Hazel . . . since there's no train there."

"I know that," the conductor said rather sharply. "I just wanted to make sure that someone would be here to meet you, Miss. This is a lonely part of the land." He shook his head as he left with the stub of Nellie's ticket.

It was August 16, 1890, and almost a year since Nellie had begun taking classes at the Winnipeg Normal School. Now she had her teaching certificate and was replacing her best friend from Normal, Annie Dale, who had taught at Hazel School from February until the end of June. Annie was quite unlike Mrs. Dale back home — and no relation. As the years went by, Mrs. Dale grew paler and thinner until now she was a gaunt woman. She looked past forty although she was only in her twenties.

Nellie stood up and bent her head to see out the window. At that point, the wheels gave a sharp, screeching sound, and she was thrown against the seat in front of her. She clung to it for a couple of seconds as the train jolted to an abrupt stop. With her alligator bag in hand, she hurried along the narrow aisle and then down the steps and onto the platform of fresh unpainted wood, which now held only her tin trunk. Even with all her belongings, the trunk was only half full, and it looked small on the empty platform.

Nellie looked up and was surprised to notice that she was surrounded by bush. She strained to see beyond the thick growth of poplar trees and soft maples and was relieved to spot a farmhouse through an opening. It was only about a mile away. She sat down on the rounded lid of her trunk and waved at the conductor. He had taken his place on the back platform of the train, which was already starting to move east along the tracks. The whistle made a lonely sound as the train picked up speed and disappeared from sight, but she could still hear the clattering of the wheels on the rails.

The trunk top was starting to feel uncomfortable, so Nellie jumped off it and walked over to sit on the edge of the platform. She swung her legs back and forth, listening to the mosquitoes that had suddenly started to swarm around her. She swatted at them as she peered along the grassy trail leading south from the stop. There was no one in sight and no sound of anyone approaching.

"Now, Nellie," Mother had said as the family saw Nellie

off at the new train station at Wawanesa, "you are out in the world. Don't talk but listen and don't believe all you hear, and don't be afraid to admit you do not know. And remember, no matter what happens to you, you can always come home and be welcome."

Nellie shivered a little, even though it was a hot day, and took out one of the three oranges that Mr. Storey, the grocery store owner in Wawanesa, had given her today when he heard that she was leaving for her first school. She dug her thumb into the thick skin of the orange and quickly peeled it. Then she pulled it apart and popped a whole section into her mouth. It was particularly sweet, and she started to feel better almost at once.

She thought about her friend, Annie, who had recommended her for this job when she had given up the post to take a school near her home. Annie and Nellie had become close friends while they were both strangers in Winnipeg. Annie was a quiet, plump, cheerful girl with cheeks as rosy as Nellie's. She had always wanted to be a teacher and, like Nellie, was concerned for farm children and their mothers who could not read. She and Nellie had spent many evenings studying together and sometimes went on outings, too.

Nellie remembered particularly the evening that she had gone with Annie to hear the Reverend Alexander Grant at First Baptist Church. Though Nellie had always been a Methodist, she was deeply moved by the church service and overcome by her past sins — especially her lying about Nap and the cows' tails. After the meeting on the way home, she and Annie discussed the service, and Annie explained to her how to pray and be saved from her sin. Nellie had come to admire Annie's unselfish life and wanted to be just like her.

When they reached Annie's little room, they had

prayed together, and Nellie finally felt certain that God had forgiven her. From that time on, her desire to help poor and underprivileged women grew even stronger. Though she remained a Methodist, Nellie still remembered the rousing message in the Baptist Church that evening and the quiet talk and prayers with Annie afterwards.

Nellie swatted at a few more mosquitoes and wondered where her ride was. Mr. Hornsberg, the Hazel School trustee, was supposed to meet her.

Nellie thought back to the farewell message that the principal of the Normal School had given at graduation. "Demand decent salaries," he had said, "and wear clean linen." So here she was waiting in her clean linen — with no one to make any demands of! Well, she was glad to be earning a salary of her own so she could pay Hannah back. She would earn forty dollars a month — all of it sheer profit, as her room and board would be provided by a member of the school board; that is, if Mr. Hornsberg ever appeared along that trail.

Nellie glanced over to the southeast, where the house was. She sighed and looked back along the trail. It seemed as though she had been there for hours but suspected that it might not be more than an hour. But she couldn't be sure, for she did not own a watch and she had never been expert at telling time from the sun. Then she heard the sound of creaking wheels and before long a buckboard came into view on the trail from the south.

A team of large, sweating Bays came right up close to the platform. Then a big, fair-haired man, who must have been in his early forties, stood up as he pulled the reins taut and the horses came to an abrupt stop. "Has the train come in?" he asked anxiously, peering beyond Nellie to the lone trunk on the platform.

"It certainly has," Nellie shot back.

The man ignored her disgruntled tone and continued. "Did you see a teacher get off that train, Miss?"

Nellie stood and stretched to her full height of just under five feet and stared at him with stern brown eyes.

"I've come to meet the new teacher for our school," the man went on. "I've taken all this time to come here to get her and she hasn't come. It's no easy job, I can tell you, being a trustee, and trying to get along with teachers. We had a fine teacher last year. But Annie Dale got herself a school back near her home, and we lost her. And now this new one doesn't even show up. I guess she missed the train or got cold feet. Now what am I to do? The children will all be at school on Monday and waiting. I ask you what am I to do? This is my last year on the school board and am I glad! I'll never let myself get cornered into this job again."

Nellie stared at the man's angry, sunburnt face. Did he really not recognize that she was the teacher?

"I'm sorry for you," she said, "but maybe you could give me a lift. I've missed meeting someone, too. I was supposed to be met by a Mr. Hornsberg, a trustee for the Hazel School, and here I've sat waiting for well over an hour."

The man blinked in amazement, then jumped onto the platform beside Nellie. He put out a big hand and said, "I'm Mr. Hornsberg. My apologies, Miss Mooney, but I swear I didn't think you could be a day over fifteen. It never dawned on me that you'd be the teacher."

Nellie gave him her most sophisticated smile as she extended her hand, but he rushed off to put her trunk onto the back of the buckboard. Then he got up into the front and held out a hand to her. Nellie stepped up with her head held high and sat on the seat next to his.

He turned the horses around and slapped them lightly, and they were off.

Nellie folded her hands in her lap and tried to look as mature as possible.

The road soon came to a small settlement. "This is St. Léon — a French village," Mr. Hornsberg said. The houses, set close together on one street, were all alike — whitewashed, with bright blue doors. Children played in the yards and street, and a number of dogs came out to chase their buckboard.

Mr. Hornsberg drove very carefully to avoid the dogs and children. "These are fine people," he said, "industrious folk. Look at those gardens behind their houses, and those fields back of them. Good, eh?"

Nellie nodded as she looked out at the fields of tall, golden wheat and shorter white-topped, bearded barley. She sighed and thought of the busy time they would be having at home with the crops almost ready to harvest.

"Well, take a good look, for it's the last good crop you'll see for a while. Folks down our way have all been hailed out. We'll get cattle feed, but that's all. It's enough to make a person turn Catholic! Beats me how they were all spared. Maybe in the fall when I have time, I'll turn Catholic. Of course, it'd be time-consuming, what with beads and confession, and early mass and prayers. By the way, we won't be able to pay you. But we'll keep you even though you don't look like much of a teacher. And we'll feed you, and you'll get your room and board free. So you better eat up, for I'm afraid that's all we'll be able to pay you for a while."

Before Nellie could react to this statement, they turned into a laneway leading to a large log cabin. There was a low flat stoop by the front door and white geraniums blooming in beds at the sides and front.

"Here we are, then," Mr. Hornsberg said. They went around to the back and a fair-haired woman came through the doorway and stood on the wooden stoop. She smiled widely at Nellie as she came up the steps. "Welcome to our home, Miss Mooney," she said with a German accent. Behind her Nellie could see a girl about her own size. It was difficult to tell how old.

"I've a meal waiting for you, but first my daughter, Esther, will show you to your room. You must be tired after that long trip. I hope you didn't have to wait too long."

Nellie smiled and shook hands with Mrs. Hornsberg while Mr. Hornsberg lifted her trunk down from the buckboard and left it on the back stoop. Two boys about ten and twelve years old, probably his sons, jumped on the wagon as Mr. Hornsberg drove the team to the barn.

Nellie stepped into the kitchen behind Mrs. Hornsberg. Esther smiled up at her with big blue eyes. She looked almost exactly like her mother — but with golden hair flowing down her back instead of being fastened around her head like her mother's.

The kitchen smelled of freshly baked bread and spicy apple pie. Pink and white geraniums sat on the ledges of three large sparkling windows. The stove shone bright black, and a flood of sunlight spilled onto the cloth on the long kitchen table. A rocking chair with brown chintz cushions stood beside a padded couch of the same colour. A knitting basket sat on the floor between them. Mrs. Hornsberg's life must be easier, Nellie thought, than many farmers' wives. It certainly would be easier than Mrs. Dale's.

"Here, come with me," Esther said, taking Nellie by the arm. She led her out of the kitchen and into a large dining room. There were flowers in all the windows there, too.

"I am fifteen," Esther said, as they left the dining room and entered a large bright room. "This is really my room, but I have to give it to the teacher. If you don't mind, though, could I stay here, too? We have a cot that we could move in for me. I would give you the big bed. I'm very quiet. Do you think we could share the room? You can't be too much older. In fact, we've never had such a young teacher before."

"I'm almost seventeen," Nellie said, "and I would be happy to share the room with you."

****

"I am your new teacher and my name is Miss Mooney." A hand shot up. "Yes?" she said.

"Is that spelled like the moon?" a red-headed young boy asked with a mischievous grin. Titters of laughter rang out around him.

Nellie sighed. Teaching her first class was going to be hard. From where she stood behind her desk on the raised platform at the front of the room, she could see that most of the students were paying attention. But two boys at the back seemed to be carving into their desks, and a couple of younger boys in front of them were pushing each other back and forth almost out of their seats. On the other side of the room two girls were talking and giggling. A lot of the students had not shut their eyes during the Lord's Prayer either.

She could not believe such rude behaviour on the first day of school, but she held back her temper and turned to write her name on the blackboard. Just then she heard a sharp cry from behind her and, as she twirled swiftly around, she saw one of the little girls holding her hand over the side of her face.

"What is the matter?" Nellie asked.

"He hit me with a spitball, Miss."

"Who hit you?" Nellie asked.

Silence filled the room. Then Nellie remembered the unwritten code of all schools: "Thou must not snitch."

"Are you all right, now?"

"Yes," the girl said in a timid voice.

Nellie did not pursue the matter further, but this time she did not take her eyes off the class as she backed cautiously to the board and wrote her name with her hand stretched sideways. A new rule came to mind. "Never turn your back on a new class." It was funny that the Normal School had never taught her that.

She was thankful that she had put the lessons on the blackboard before the pupils had arrived. And so many had come, because there was no harvest this year. Normally, they would have been needed at home to help with the threshing.

Nellie reseated the students together into classes as she learned the name and grade level of each. "This way, you'll be able to help each other," she said loudly, above the giggles of some of the older girls, who were now placed near the young men in their class and didn't seem to mind at all. The boys still continued to scowl from the back row. She knew that they thought the way Jack used to and would rather have been home. She vowed to keep them coming to school so they would not be sorry later.

It wasn't hard for Nellie to tell when recess had come. Heads had started turning and one little boy in the front row was waving his hand frantically and pointing to the clock on the back wall.

Nellie just smiled at him and nodded. "It is recess time," she announced. "You will have fifteen minutes. There will be a warning bell three minutes ahead so that you can line up to file back inside. Class dismissed."

There was a mad rush and cries and shouts as the children pushed and shoved their way through the single doorway. Nellie groaned as she watched, but before she could get up, they were all outside — all, that is, except Esther, who stood beside her desk.

Esther raised her large, sympathetic blue eyes and said, "May I help you put some lessons on the board for after recess?"

Nellie sighed and grabbed her scribbler of prepared lessons. She and Esther would have only fifteen minutes to get this all on the board before the pupils came back.

They were halfway through when Nellie heard a loud cry. "Come quick, Miss Moon, come quick." A girl stood in the doorway, her lips trembling. "It's the big boys. Ned and Dan are fighting." Nellie handed her scribbler to Esther and rushed ahead of the little girl and out the door.

The children were all gathered in a circle. Nellie nudged her way through to see what was holding their attention so closely. Two of the bigger boys were lashing out at each other with their fists, and one already had blood trickling from his nose.

"That's Ned with the bloody nose," the little girl said. "He and Dan hate each other."

Nellie noticed that the boys seemed to be about the same size — one was a little taller but the other was fatter. Nellie decided just to watch. If she stopped them now, they would fight it out on the way home. Wouldn't it be better to get it over now under supervision?

Nellie was amazed at the red-faced fury of the boys as they struck out at each other. Ned caught Dan by the arm and flipped him over on his back. Then Ned jumped on Dan even though blood was spurting out of his nose onto the boy beneath him. But suddenly the fatter boy brought up his legs and sent Ned sprawling on his back a few feet away. Then they were both on their feet again glaring at each other. Dan was now bleeding, too — from a cut on the side of his head. The fresh blood trickled through his straw-coloured hair.

Nellie realized now that she had to stop this fight. But how was she going to do that? They would never pay attention to her commands, and might accidentally knock her sprawling if she stepped between them.

Nellie turned to the little girl by her side. "Run inside and bring me back my bell," Nellie ordered. "Quick now."

A few moments later Nellie stood on the stoop with the bell in hand, flinging her arm up and down in a wide half-circle. She kept ringing it loudly up and down as it had probably never been rung before.

Slowly but surely the group started to break up and the children formed a line to enter the school. Then Nellie saw a sight she would never forget. At the end of the line, with heads bent, the two bedraggled fighters, leaning against each other for support, limped up the steps and into the school. Nellie decided to ignore their condition.

****

Finally four o'clock came, and Nellie asked the pupils to stand for dismissal. She had forgotten to start an orderly routine, and as they jammed the door as before, she did not worry about the commotion. The younger ones seemed to know enough to stand back and let the older, stronger ones go first, and so no one was hurt. Swiftly, the room was empty and a glorious silence followed. Nellie could hear only the distant sound of shouting children and barking dogs.

Nellie had never been so tired in her whole life. She felt as if she had swum for miles and miles and just crawled up on shore. She saw only dear Esther, who had stayed to help write the next day's lessons on the board. Nellie lay her arms and head on the desk in complete exhaustion.

Only then did she hear a timid "Miss . . . Miss." She could not believe the voices were still echoing in her head. She lay still. She was more tired than she thought.

"Miss . . . Miss." A bony finger poked her arm.

Nellie jerked upright. There stood Jimmy Burns from the Junior Second Class — one of the children she had seated on the front platform in the afternoon, so she could be sure they completed their work. She suspected that he was the one who had bounced the spitball off the little girl's cheek. Just now, though, his twinkling brown eyes had become very serious as he looked at her. He was shaking his shaggy head of thick brown hair in bewilderment as he asked, "You weren't asleep, were you, Miss?

"Oh, no." Nellie managed a smile.

"Miss, I've a note from Ma." He pushed his hand inside his trousers and pulled out a crumpled paper. He pulled a wad of sticky spruce gum off the ball and then handed the note to her.

Nellie unfolded the note and read it silently.

Dear Miss Mooney,

Would you please cut Jimmy's hair? He looks a mess, but I just can't get around to it. And I reckon you won't mind since you got so much more time than any of the rest of us farm women.

Mrs. Burns

Nellie stared at the note in disbelief. She remembered her resolve to help farm women, but she hadn't counted on this!

Nellie looked up at the boy. "Your mother wants *me* to cut your hair?"

He looked back at her solemnly. "Yes, and my pa says you'll probably make a good job of it, too."

"But I don't even know if there are scissors here!" Nellie opened the low, flat middle drawer of the desk and reached inside.

"Oh, sure there are," Jimmy said. "The last teacher always kept them at the back of that drawer so's the younger children couldn't reach them when they got into her desk."

Nellie reached into the dark recesses of her desk and, sure enough, her hand felt a large pair of scissors. She drew them out slowly. But she had never cut anyone's hair before.

"You'll need to sit up here so I can see all around your head." Jimmy nimbly hitched himself up on the side of the desk.

"Here," said Esther, who had stopped writing on the board to watch. "Tie my apron around his neck, so the hair won't get all over his clothes."

"I'll have to wash your hair first," Nellie said, staring at the boy's matted locks.

The boy screwed his nose up, so his face looked all wrinkled. But then he said, "That's okay, Miss."

"Esther, would you mind bringing me a pail of water from the barrel outside. There's nothing like soft rain water for washing hair."

Esther came back quickly with the water, and with one hand on Jimmy's head and the other on the soft soap, Nellie asked Esther to fill the tin basin on the wooden stand just inside the door.

After Jimmy's hair was soaped twice and rinsed thoroughly, Nellie brought him to the front desk again and dabbed his hair with some toilet water from her purse.

"That sure smells nice," he said. "I bet tomorrow all the kids will want to stay after school to have their hair cut."

Somewhat numbly, Nellie took Esther's apron from her desk and wrapped it around the boy's small neck. They had never prepared her for this in Normal School, she thought again. As she raised the scissors to start cutting, the boy smiled at her.

"Please, Miss, do you think you could cut it curly?"

19

"She's the only woman I've ever met that I'd want for a mother-in-law," Nellie said. Somehow she had survived the first two weeks of school and was now eating her Saturday noon meal with the Hornsbergs.

They were shocked at what Nellie had just said and stared at her in silence. Nellie was talking about the wife of the new Methodist minister. She and her husband had been at Hazel for only a month, and Nellie had met her just once — at the Young Ladies' Bible Class.

Mr. Hornsberg broke into a loud laugh and his sons, Charley and Fred, followed his example. Mrs. Hornsberg smiled and said, "I'm afraid Mrs. McClung could not be your mother-in-law, Nellie. Her sons are too young for you!"

"Oh," Nellie said in a subdued tone. "How old are they?"

"Ten and fourteen."

"Well, I'm not quite seventeen. And anyway what's three years? When he's fifty, I don't think he'll mind that I'm fifty-three. And why aren't they in school?"

"They go to school in Manitou, where the manse is. The minister has two charges — one at Hazel and one at Manitou."

Mr. Hornsberg laughed loudly again, and the others smiled. They liked this new teacher who kept life interesting for those around her. One thing was certain — they never knew what she would say next. Nellie had completely forgotten her mother's warning not to talk too much.

There was a knock then, and Mrs. Hornsberg put down her serviette and walked over to the front door.

"Oh, dear!" Nellie exclaimed. "That must be Isabel Smith to take me to Mrs. Brown's quilting bee. I'd better hurry." Nellie jumped from the table and rushed into her bedroom. Isabel Smith, a teacher from Manitou who had gone to Normal School with Hannah, had invited her to go to this bee at the Browns' near Hazel. Nellie had been only too happy to accept the invitation. She hoped she would have a chance to talk to Isabel about some of the problems she had in handling students.

It was a balmy September day, so the girls had decided to walk the mile to the Browns'. The smell of golden rod and wild sage was in the air. In the field near the road, Mr. Hornsberg's plough still stood where he had unhitched the team to go to dinner. He was turning under the stubble left after he had harvested the remains of the hailed-out wheat. The earth looked rich and brown and gave promise of good crops again. The Hornsbergs were not in want in spite of this disaster, for they had harvested a two-year supply each of the previous four years. "Hailed out one year in five is not too bad," Mr. Hornsberg had said. "We really can't complain."

"How do you like teaching?" Isabel asked, once they were on the road to Hazel. She gave Nellie that mature, self-confident smile that comes only after three years of success as a teacher.

Nellie cringed. She would not ask Isabel any questions after all, for Hannah's friend might just guess what a dismal failure she really was. She turned to Isabel and said, "Oh, I love it. Time just flies." Well, the last part was right, she thought.

"My beginners are so darling, and the bigger ones help all the time," Isabel said. "This is my best class. They're a joy to teach."

Nellie looked at her and almost choked. She thought of her own classes and her own failure. The two weeks had been pure torture. Nothing had gone right, it seemed. She had dragged out Baldwin's *School Management* from the bottom of her trunk to find a solution. It had been much used and highly recommended by her Normal School teachers, but it had no answers for the problems she was facing now.

Part of the difficulty was that she had to prepare so many lessons. With eight grades and several subjects for every grade, how could anyone find enough hours in the night to prepare them all? And children who were not busy always found a way to disrupt the class.

Another difficulty was that most of the families came from the same community in Ontario. They had brought old feuds with them and passed them on to their children. This led to repeated fights in the school yard. Nellie was hesitant to take a firm stand with pupils almost as old as and bigger than herself so she had gone to Baldwin for advice. She had searched through his book for feuds, fights, quarrels, and even vendettas — and found no such listings. Obviously, Baldwin had never taught in a place like Hazel. She thought about appealing to the school board but decided against it. Some of the trustees were not speaking to each other, since they also came from the same place in Ontario.

The passing clouds cast dark blue shadows over the fields. Nellie and Isabel walked on in silence, and before long, they reached the Brown homestead. They walked up the verandah steps and knocked on the oak front door.

"Come in, come in," Mrs. Brown said, a smile spreading across her kindly face as she opened the door. She was a plump, jolly woman, and Nellie was glad she had come. It would be good to forget about her school problems for a while.

She and Isabel followed Mrs. Brown into the dining room, where she had set up the quilting frame, which was about six feet wide and eight feet long. To make room for it, all the boards had been taken from the dining room table and placed against the hall doorway.

A group of women were already seated around the quilt, which had been stretched in the frame. The four corners were held firmly with clamps, and the edges tacked to the boards all the way around. The frame was supported on the backs of four chairs. The dozen ladies sat on stools they had brought with them.

The women guided their needles through the layers of cloth and wool batting. The stitching had to be fine to make the quilt last for generations to come.

"We're doing a Bethlehem Star pattern," Mrs. Brown said proudly. "It's to be a gift for the manse for Christmas. We're well ahead of schedule this year, since there's not been the usual heavy harvest, but we're happy to have extra hands to help. Now come on out to the kitchen first and have a cup of tea and a bite to eat."

Nellie followed willingly, for she had not yet finished her dinner when Isabel had arrived. On the kitchen table were freshly baked lemon meringue and apple pies; tarts of all kinds: butter syrup, pumpkin, raspberry, mincemeat, and raisin; and piles of fluffy, sugar-coated, fried donuts, slices of fresh bread, and rolled cinnamon buns next to a bowl of rich yellow butter and a jar of wild strawberry preserves.

"Just help yourselves, ladies," Mrs. Brown said as she poured two cups of tea.

Nellie chose a thick slice of fresh bread and covered it with the butter and wild strawberry jam. Isabel just sat and sipped her tea. "I'd like to eat something, but I don't want to gain any more weight. Teaching seems to agree with me. I've gained a few pounds."

"I don't know what I weigh now," Nellie said, "but when I left home I weighed ninety-five pounds. So I'm not worried. Still, I'm short; so someday I might have to worry about being fat, I suppose."

Isabel seemed to bristle a bit. "Well, I'm going to join the ladies." She got up and walked into the other room, leaving Nellie eating her jam and bread by herself, since Mrs. Brown had already gone to join the women. Nellie was in no hurry to join the others, for she was not a fast quilter. Under Lizzie's patient tutoring, she had finally learned to use a needle passably, but she knew she would never be a great seamstress. She reached for a piece of lemon pie and wondered if it would be as good as her mother's. It wasn't, but it was not bad — better than she could make. She ate each mouthful slowly and listened to the conversation drifting out from the other room.

"Can you believe it?" one voice said. "She and this other lady from Manitou are going around taking names for their cause."

"Who?"

"What cause?"

"Mrs. McClung, the new minister's wife. I don't know who the other woman is."

"What are they collecting names for?"

Nellie could hear the needles clicking against thimbles as the ladies talked.

"You won't believe this, but they are trying to get women to ask for the vote. Can you imagine!"

"The vote!"

"Yes, she's trying to get women to sign a petition."

"Maybe, she's just being kind to this other woman."

"Well, if that's the case, she should have more backbone . . . being a minister's wife and all, one expects more."

"I don't think you're right there, Sarah," Mrs. Brown said. "I think she's the one who's doing the pushing. I heard rumours that she tried doing something like this back in Ontario. Maybe that's why folks let them leave and we got such a fine minister. It's a shame how some wives can be such a trial to men."

"Well, I can't think she'd have the nerve to come here to our quilting bee and ask *us* to sign."

"Well, I certainly won't sign it if she asks me," Mrs. Wheeler said. "It would be an insult to my husband." Nellie could hear the women clicking their tongues in agreement even though Mrs. Wheeler's husband was known to be the neighbourhood drunk.

Mrs. Wheeler had introduced herself to Nellie two days before. She had waddled up to the Hazel school at about ten o'clock in the morning to enroll her five-year-old boy in the primer class. She had wanted to leave her two little girls, aged four and three, as well. But Nellie had refused to let them come.

So Mrs. Wheeler had left somewhat flustered, carrying her one-year-old boy, while her two girls helped their two-year-old brother. Nellie could see that another baby would be arriving soon.

At noon that day, Esther had whispered to Nellie that Mrs. Wheeler was the wife of the neighbourhood drunk. Not that people in town objected to folks drinking once in a while, but this man drank through *all* the seasons. And there was a difference, Esther said, between a winter and a summer drinker. No decent farmer ever drank at harvest time — but Mr. Wheeler did.

Nellie was jarred back to the present by a sharp knock on the kitchen door. The women were so busy chatting that Mrs. Brown didn't hear the knock, so Nellie opened the door.

"Why, Mrs. McClung!" Nellie almost gasped, knowing how unwelcome she would be. In a second, though, she said, "Do come in, ladies."

As Mrs. McClung and her companion stepped into the kitchen, Mrs. Brown came out of the dining room and closed the door behind her, but Nellie could still hear the quilters' rustling skirts and giggling. The sound of light footsteps pattering up the stairs and overhead left no doubt about where the ladies had gone.

"Mrs. McClung and Sarah Jones, do come and have a cup of tea," Mrs. Brown said politely, but there was a chill in her tone.

The ladies sat down quietly as Mrs. Brown poured the tea and handed it to Mrs. McClung and the other lady, who was a younger woman, perhaps in her mid-thirties. Nellie noticed that she did not wear a wedding ring.

Mrs. McClung smiled at Nellie, and Nellie smiled back, then kept staring at this striking woman in her late forties. She was dressed in a brown cashmere dress with a finely smocked yoke and cuffs. Her spotless white linen collar was held in place by a moonstone brooch. On her rich brown hair, she had set a dark golden velvet bonnet trimmed with lighter coloured folds of silk. It set off her large, sensitive brown eyes beautifully.

Mrs. McClung was looking at Mrs. Brown with quiet confidence as she began speaking: "We have come to ask for signatures for our petition. It is . . ."

"I know," Mrs. Brown said. "You are asking us to go against our own husbands and sign a petition to give women the vote."

"You need not go against your husband, Mrs. Brown. If you had the vote, you might strengthen his vote by casting yours for the same person. However, you would have a choice. Right now, you have none."

"Well, my husband handles matters like that and he does just fine. I see no reason to meddle in men's affairs." Mrs. Brown got up and opened the dining room door. There was no sign of the others, but it was obvious that they had been there. Even Isabel had disappeared. Several spools of thread and various needles lay on the quilt in in the centre of the room.

"Perhaps some of the ladies at your quilting bee think differently, but I see they have gone." There were rustling sounds from the back stairway, but Mrs. McClung did not seem to notice. "I am so sorry I missed them," she said sweetly. "Now, Nellie, how would you feel about signing?"

"Yes, I will sign," Nellie said, gulping. "I have always thought that women should have the vote. It was a great shock to me when I found out that they did not have it."

Nellie knew that she would have to face the wrath of the others afterwards, but she didn't care. Mrs. McClung was right! And besides, she was a fine lady. There was not a woman there who was as gracious and well-spoken as Mrs. McClung in her modest but stylish clothes.

As Nellie signed her name, she noticed that there was only one other name above hers on the petition. She handed the pen back to Mrs. McClung in silence.

The two women left quickly, and Nellie felt a sense of panic as the ladies returned to the room. Even Isabel was shocked to hear that she had signed, and the others stared at her in disbelief. In a short time, everyone had settled back to quilting, but not before making more nasty remarks about Mrs. McClung.

When they had quilted all around the four sides of the quilt as far as they could reach, Mrs. Brown said, "Well, ladies, I always say when the outside's finished, the quilt's half done." She was right, for when they folded the quilted sections under the frames so the ladies could reach the new part, the unquilted surface was much smaller. This meant there was no longer room for everyone to work.

Nellie took the opportunity to leave.

"Mrs. Brown, I have lessons to prepare for Monday. Do you mind if I leave you now?"

"Oh, not at all, dear. We wouldn't want to stand in the way of your work — since you are an independent woman."

"Thank you, Mrs. Brown. It's been a very interesting afternoon."

Isabel did not leave with Nellie. In fact, she seemed to be keeping her distance as much as possible.

As Nellie walked the mile home, she wondered why these good women were being so mean. If Mrs. McClung had approached any one of them alone, they would have treated her with respect and hospitality, even though they likely would not have signed the petition. But together, they couldn't say enough mean things about her. One nasty remark seemed to lead to another. Was it because they were in a crowd?

****

"It's possible you could have your mother-in-law, after all," Mrs. Hornsberg said as she passed Nellie the scalloped potatoes. They were having supper the Friday after the bee, and Nellie had been relaxing and looking forward to the weekend. But at this news, she sat up straight and stared at Mrs. Hornsberg.

"The McClungs have an eighteen-year-old son," Mrs. Hornsberg said.

"They do?" Nellie's eyes opened wide.

"Yes. He arrived this week and he's working in the drug store in Manitou, but . . . he has red hair."

"I've always liked red hair," Nellie blurted out, and she did, though she had never realized it until just that minute.

The Hornsbergs all smiled and were not too surprised the next afternoon when Nellie decided to hitch up the sorrel and ride over to Manitou.

She wore her best dark green dress, trimmed with military braid and gold buttons. Her shoes shone from a fresh application of lard and lamp black. She had waved her hair with curling papers the night before, and her cheeks, normally quite rosy, were even pinker than usual by the time she got to Manitou. She had been pinching them at regular intervals all the way.

Nellie tied her horse to the hitching post, marched into the small store, and looked for a man with red hair. She was not disappointed, for he was the only person in the store.

"May I help you?" he said, leaning on the counter and resting his chin in one hand.

Nellie looked straight into his large blue eyes. He was tall and slim and had his mother's fine features and clear skin.

Nellie had to think fast to make up a reason for being there. He kept staring at her.

"I came to buy a . . ." She looked down at the counter, and there right beside the till was a display of pens. ". . . a pen. I need another one. A teacher always needs a good pen." She took one from the display, removed the cap, and carefully examined the split nib.

"I'm Wes McClung, by the way," the red-headed man said.

Nellie smiled and extended her hand across the counter. "Welcome to Manitou, Wes McClung. I'm Nellie Mooney, the new schoolteacher in Hazel, just next door. So I guess we have something in common. We're both new to the community."

He returned her friendly smile. "They're both nice little towns," he said. "Different than Port Arthur, where we lived before."

Nellie wasn't sure he would still think it nice if he knew about all the feuds and his mother's reception at the quilting bee. Wes waited patiently for her to choose a pen, still smiling.

"May I try one, please?" Nellie asked.

Wes reached behind the counter and brought out a used pen like the one Nellie was holding. He handed it to her, along with a fresh sheet of paper. Then he took the lid off a bottle of blue ink sitting on the counter.

Nellie dipped her pen in the ink and started to scroll her name and address very legibly on the paper. Then Wes said, "Those pens are a real bargain for the price, but we have fountain pens at three dollars each if you would care to see them."

Nellie watched as Wes went to a side shelf and unlocked a case that held jewellery and other items. He brought a small tray of pens to the counter and set it in front of her.

"Real fountain pens! They're beautiful," Nellie said, captivated by the shades of sapphire, emerald, and ruby. She had always wanted to own a fountain pen and had never seen such exquisite pieces.

"They write beautifully, too," Wes said.

Nellie did not fill the new pen but dipped the fine point into the ink and started to write. *My favourite author is Charles Dickens because he is a voice for the voiceless, a defender of the weak, a flaming fire . . .*

Nellie felt her hand go off the line as Mrs. Brown brushed in beside her and leaned against the counter. "I've waited long enough, young man. While she's writing a letter to someone there, I'd like some service. And so would these other folks who've been waiting." She stared at them both with lips tight and eyes narrowed a little.

Wes and Nellie looked up, startled by Mrs. Brown's comment, but sure enough, two other ladies were waiting near the counter. Wes looked a little uneasy but said nothing.

"I love the pen. I'll take it," Nellie said. She handed three dollars to Wes and turned to Mrs. Brown. "I won't be a minute now that I've decided. I'm sorry to have held you up. I didn't know you were waiting."

Wes took the money and put the pen back in its own

little box. It was the same colour as the pen. Then he wrapped it in brown paper and handed it to Nellie.

"It's a beautiful pen," Nellie said. "Thank you for showing it to me. And it was nice meeting you."

Wes smiled a friendly, beaming smile, and his blue eyes lit up as he said, "I hope to see you again, Miss Mooney."

Nellie gave him her most encouraging smile, and then with head held high, she turned and whisked by Mrs. Brown and the other two women. Under her arm, Nellie had tucked her purse that now held the best pen she had ever seen but not a cent. She'd spent everything she had.

20

Nellie sat on a flat rock not far from the Hazel School. It was Friday afternoon and she was feeling very badly about teaching. It was not at all as she had imagined it would be. The pupils fought every day at noon hour and often pushed and shoved one another as they came back to class. She was powerless, it seemed, to stop them.

What if the inspector was to come and see her lack of control over the students? Isabel had said that he always came early to assess the first-year teachers, but Nellie certainly wasn't ready for him yet.

Cowbells tingled in the distance, and for a moment Nellie wished she was still tending the cattle in the pasture back home. Then she would not have to face the problems of a community like Hazel. She must think of something, for she did not want to go home in disgrace.

Nellie stared back at the pale grey frame schoolhouse. It was set well back from the road and had a black roof. A lone Manitoba maple grew in the middle of the large front yard — the students' fighting ground.

Suddenly an idea come to Nellie. What the children needed was a new game to play — one that would take their attention away from old feuds. Perhaps it might even give their parents something new to talk about! She didn't know what it would be, but she would think of something, and she did have forty dollars. The trustees had been able to pay her, after all. She reached into her pocket to feel the bills again.

The chirping of crickets in the long grass nearby mingled with the quiet drone of mowers. The farmer next to the school was cutting a second-growth crop of alfalfa. The soft light of the setting sun cast a pleasant warmth around her as she stood up and turned towards home. A good supper would be waiting for her there. She was already starting to feel better.

****

"We're going to play a new game," Nellie announced to her class at noon hour the following day. She had asked them to meet here by the front steps of the school. And, sure enough, it seemed that they had all been curious enough to come. A few were still eating their lunch. Nellie held up an inflated rubber ball covered with brown cowskin.

"It's a football," big Ned Harkness shouted. Then, pulling a piece of grass through his teeth, he emitted a screeching whistle. But it was the first time he had ever volunteered an answer, so Nellie smiled back at him.

Mary Wheeler, one of the smaller girls seated on the

bottom step, said, "But, Miss, girls never play football. It's too rough for girls."

"Well, the girls don't have to take part, but they can if they want to. Sometimes I may join in, too. Have any of you ever played football before?"

"Naw, they didn't play that back where I came from," a boy said as he pushed his dark brown hair out of his eyes and came a little closer to stare even harder at the ball.

Frank Jeffreys was waving his hand. "I saw the Manitou team playing one day last year. It looked like fun."

Nellie picked up the slate she had brought out. "Since we're all new at the game, I would like us to make our own rules. Who would like to write them down for us?"

"Me," shouted a half dozen students.

Nellie chose Jim Andrews and handed him a fresh piece of chalk from her pocket. She would have liked to pick Frank, who stood off by himself, but she didn't, for Frank was quiet and did not mingle much with the other children. And she knew that the children would only be jealous if she picked him. He had enough problems to face with his mother, Mrs. Jeffreys, the neigbourhood gossip. She had only the one son. Her three step-children were already away from home, and she had time on her hands.

The big boys were mumbling among themselves. Would they walk away now? Nellie wondered.

"Boys . . . and girls, I would like a few suggestions for the rules." Nellie kept staring at the boys, who were still talking.

Finally, Dan, a brown-haired young man with hazel-green eyes, brushed by a group of older girls to come nearer to Nellie. "If the girls plan to play, too, I guess we won't be able to play tackle football." Howls of laughter came from the rest of the boys, while the older girls standing to the left of the school steps stared stonily at him.

"You're right, Dan. We won't play tackle, but it's not because of the girls on the team. It's because there's such a difference in everyone's age and size," Nellie explained patiently. "We'll play like the English. First, we'll set up our goal markers and choose sides."

"Will we choose sides like in baseball?"

"I prefer a different method. We'll choose sides by alphabet and by class. That way, half of each grade will be on one team and half will be on the other."

Nellie was pleased to see Frank come over to the side where Jim held the slate and say in a low voice, "Do you think, Miss Mooney, that we could play against the Manitou team sometime?"

"I don't see why not. But let's get playing among ourselves first."

By now, they were all ready to start, so in ten minutes the rules were completed.

The aim of the game was to kick the ball through the opposing team's goal. Three of the posts were sticks from the woodshed; the other was the trunk of the maple tree. The players could kick the ball with their feet only. And they could kick it no higher than the goalkeeper's head. If they did, it would be out of bounds. They could not use their hands to pass the ball to a teammate. Some suggested that they should be able to use their heads for hitting the ball, but Nellie promptly discouraged this idea. She could too easily picture two children jumping up to hit the ball this way and colliding. The bigger player would squash the smaller one.

"After we choose sides, let's practise a while," Nellie

said. "That way, we'll know who can play best in certain places."

A few girls sat on the school steps, not moving. Other pupils eagerly waited their turn to have a chance to kick the ball between the lines of the far goal — the wooden post and the trunk of the maple tree.

****

Three weeks later, Nellie and her class picked who would form a Hazel School team and play a game against Manitou School. Nellie and Mr. Holmes, a Manitou teacher, had negotiated the rules to make them uniform.

Nellie wondered if Hazel could possibly stand against Manitou's all boys' team, which had played and won five games out of eight last fall. This September, they had been coached by Mr. Holmes, an Englishman who had immigrated to Canada. It was rumoured that he had played professional football across the sea.

Mr. Holmes had won out against Nellie's rule about not heading the ball and Nellie felt uneasy. Perhaps she should have limited the games to their own school. Perhaps she should not have allowed the girls to play along with the boys. But then she remembered her own experience racing at the picnic.

So here they were on a Friday afternoon in their own school yard, playing against a tough-looking team. Five of the Manitou players, all bigger than any Hazel member, except Ned and Frank, sat on the school steps with their long legs stretched out across the lawn. The whole west side of the school ground was filled with their classmates. The whole school must have come to see them win against the Hazel pupils, gathered across the playing field. A brisk wind wafted a few more yellow maple leaves across the school yard and under the feet of both sides.

The first goal of the game had been scored by Esther on a low hard shot from a difficult angle. The Hazel players had come to expect such a play from Esther these past few weeks, but it had taken the opposition by surprise today. There was a lot of shouting, blaming, and arguing amongst the Manitou players.

Then the Manitou team started to play with the experience Nellie expected them to display. But for all their fine passing and shooting, by the last quarter they only had one point to show for their effort. Hazel had two — a remarkable upset for the new team, Nellie thought. Manitou's goal had been scored by their fastest player, Scott Floyd. He outraced two Hazel defenders and smiled widely as he blasted a shot into the goal from twenty feet out. That smile was etched in the minds of Hazel's goaltender and everyone else at that end of the field. Just when it seemed Manitou was going to finish off this rag-tag bunch of newcomers, Ned Harkness, Hazel's oldest and biggest player, did the last thing Mr. Holmes or anyone else on the Manitou team expected — he headed a high ball past the open-mouthed Manitou goaltender. Nellie wondered where Ned had learned to head the ball, since it hadn't been allowed at school.

The goal had come early in the last quarter, and things were looking up for Hazel school. Mr. Holmes began to pace up and down the sidelines.

Nellie looked at her watch. There was now less than a minute in the game. Even if we lose, it doesn't matter, she thought. We're a rookie team — and no fights have broken out!

Then a gust of wind whipped across the field, carrying leaves with it and lifting the ball over a number of players' heads. It dropped right onto the foot of Scott Floyd, Manitou's only goal scorer in the game so far. There was no one between Scott and the Hazel's goaltender. The cheering from both schools became deafening. It looked now as if victory would slip away.

Frank Jeffreys was Hazel's goalie. His team had originally put him in goal because he was a loner and a big boy, who would not be too swift in the field. But his popularity had risen as his goaltending skills had emerged, and everyone agreed that Frank had cat-like reflexes for a boy his size. But how would this novice stand up against Scott Floyd?

Nellie clenched her fists as Frank ran out to challenge the incoming shooter.

"Get it, Frank!" she blurted out.

But Frank tripped and fell on an exposed root from the old maple-tree goalpost.

Scott Floyd smiled, and with twenty feet left to go, he kicked the ball towards the open side of the goal.

The ball shot through the air.

Then, somehow, Frank dived with outstretched arms straight across the goal, and the ball glanced off his fingertips and went wide. The whistle blew and the game was over. Hazel had won!

"Hooray for Frank," everyone shouted. Frank looked up shyly and started to rub the dirt and leaves off his bleeding knees. Then his classmates jumped off the fence and came running over to him. Ned and Charley hoisted him onto their shoulders and carried him around the playing field, calling out, "Hooray for Frank! Hooray for Hazel!"

The Hazel pupils fell back a little to allow Nellie to reach the team. Her cheeks flushed with pride and excitement as she shouted, "I knew you could do it!"

Then they yelled, "Three cheers for Miss Mooney!"

****

Nellie straightened her small felt hat and knocked again on the Jeffreys' front door. Mrs. Jeffreys opened the door and peered out. She raised her eyebrows a little at the sight of Nellie standing there, then regained her composure.

"Come in, Miss Mooney," she said pleasantly. Nellie felt she was not unwelcome. After all, Mrs. Jeffreys had told her to call anytime because they always had plenty.

"I've been intending to call," Nellie said, "ever since that day in Manitou when you invited me to come by."

"Yes, so I did. And it's a pleasure to have you. You're staying for supper, I hope."

"That would be very nice," Nellie replied, properly.

Nellie had not ridden her sorrel all the way to the Jeffreys' farm just for supper. She had come to save the football team. It had been two weeks since Hazel's victory, and there were rumours that a few mothers, led by Mrs. Jeffreys, wanted the school board to stop the games. They thought the play was too rough for the children — especially the girls. So Nellie had come to appeal to Mrs. Jeffreys, who had influence with most members of the school board. She had also reasoned that Mrs. Jeffreys would surely want the games to continue for the sake of Frank.

"Well, this is a surprise, but our honour to have the schoolteacher for supper. You know, the last teacher we had here never dropped by once. A real shame when teachers don't realize their role in the community."

"Yes, indeed," Nellie said.

"Now, we don't stand on ceremony here, so I'm

going to set you peeling the potatoes and carrots while I put out the good dishes," Mrs. Jeffreys said as she took Nellie's grey fall coat and led the way into the kitchen.

"There's the potatoes." Mrs. Jeffreys motioned Nellie over to a pan of potatoes on the side table. "But wait till I get you a pinafore to put on over that good dress."

Nellie smiled and held out her arms as Mrs. Jeffreys slipped the pinafore over her head. Nellie took the paring knife and began.

Mrs. Jeffreys raced out of the room for a few minutes and then came back with her arms full of canned preserves. She opened a jar of spiced pears and another of rich-looking applesauce. Nellie began wondering if she should speak her mind now or later.

"Mrs. Jeffreys," Nellie began, "has your son been telling you about our football games?"

Nellie felt the woman stiffen as she said, "Yes, Miss Mooney, he has."

Just then, Frank burst open the door and came inside. "Ma . . . that looks like Miss Mooney's sorrel out there." He was facing his mother and had his back to Nellie.

"Hello, Frank," Nellie said. "Your mother has invited me to stay to supper."

"Oh, hooray!"

"Here, Frank," his mother said, as she picked up a pail from the side table and emptied the remaining water into the kettle. "Run down to the well and get some water."

"I don't want to discuss football in front of Frank," Mrs. Jeffreys said when he was gone. "He's crazy about the game. Just crazy!"

"Hello, all," a voice came from the back door. It was Mr. Jeffreys, who had just come in from the field. "Well, who have we here?"

"Miss Mooney has come to visit," Mrs. Jeffreys said pleasantly.

"Well, Miss Mooney, it's a pleasure. Frank will be pleased, too. He talks so much about school these days. He never used to like it."

Mrs. Jeffreys gave her husband a cold stare and he stared down at the floor.

Before long they all sat down to a feast of roast beef, gravy, potatoes, baked beans, and pickles. Dessert followed, with cake, cookies, and pears. At first, Nellie's appetite was somewhat dulled by her mission, but it soon returned. It was true that Mrs. Jeffreys could put on a meal with no notice, just as she had said.

After a few polite enquiries about Nellie's schoolwork, Mr. Jeffreys fell silent and let his wife do the talking.

Finally, Mr. Jeffreys excused himself and Frank to go do the evening chores. Nellie knew the time had come. But first she hoped to get Mrs. Jeffreys in a pleasant frame of mind. So she started to clear the dishes and volunteered to dry them. When they were halfway through, Nellie finally said bluntly, "Mrs. Jeffreys, I want to talk about the football games."

Mrs. Jeffreys looked all over the room as if she was hunting for more dirty dishes. But there were none to be found. "Frank loves football," Nellie began, "and he is a wonderful member of the team. He's playing with others more now, and even his schoolwork is improving. He's developed a lot of self-confidence."

"But he talks of nothing else but football. He's plumb crazy over it." Mrs Jeffreys pursed her lips together tightly and stared at Nellie. "He never talks about his schoolwork anymore."

"But he's doing even better in school now. And he has friends, too."

"Does he? Or just until he misses the next goal?"

"Oh, I think now they've accepted him, it won't matter as long as he keeps trying. Anyway, he won't miss too often. He's very skilled."

"Well, my sister Carol, that's Mrs. Miller, came to me. She's concerned about her daughter."

"Girls don't have to play unless they want to."

"Oh, she wants to, all right. She's wild about the game. But it's not ladylike for the girls — kicking balls all over. It's such a rough game, too. Why I've heard mothers say their childen are coming home with dirty, ripped clothes and skinned arms and legs."

"They're no worse than they used to be! And a lot happier!" Nellie was almost shouting now, in spite of herself. "You should have seen the quarrels at noon hour and after school. It was something awful, Mrs. Jeffreys. Bloody noses and torn clothes. And the girls, too — pulling hair and biting. I just couldn't believe such fighting among children."

Mrs. Jeffreys showed no shock at Nellie's comments. She was apparently quite familiar with the situation. "Oh, well, children will be children; they often have their little squabbles. You can't expect to stop that."

"But I have stopped it . . . with the football games! Now their energy is in the game, and . . . I can control the game. I can take the ball away and stop the fighting."

"Are you admitting, Miss Mooney, that you had lost control — without football?" Mrs. Jeffreys' lips tightened into a fine line, and her beady eyes were staring straight through Nellie now.

Nellie gulped. Her horrible secret was out. And to whom had she admitted it? The community gossip. Now everyone would know that she was a failure. How could she have been so stupid as to come to this woman? But the games had been going well and so had school lately. She would try again.

"Mrs. Jeffreys, it is not my fault that the children fight over things that happened long before I came to Hazel School. They are arguing matters that their parents discuss freely in front of them. And it has not been healthy for them."

Mrs. Jeffreys was staring relentlessly at Nellie now as she slid another wet dish onto the draining tray. Nellie went on. "Why on earth should children care about a tale of how some other child's grandfather opened a registered letter twenty-five years ago and lost his job? It's so ridiculous."

A wet dish slipped from Mrs. Jeffreys' hand and broke into pieces as it hit the floor. She ignored the shattered plate and said, "It never happened. I tell you . . . it never happened. It was all a lie."

Mrs. Jeffreys looked pale and sat down while Nellie swept up the pieces.

As Nellie left the Jeffreys' house and got onto the sorrel, she had a feeling the football games would go on. And they did. Mrs. Jeffreys never brought up the topic again, and the school board never heard a single complaint.

21

Nellie stepped along briskly, for it was one of those autumn days with a rawness in the air that reminds you that snow will soon be coming. She was going to the Wheelers', who had the most run-down farm in the area. They also had six young mouths to feed and were expecting a seventh any day now. Under her arm, Nellie carried a very special parcel.

Mary Wheeler, who was in the Junior Second Class at Hazel School, was a very bright little girl, and she worked hard. She never caused trouble and was a bit shy. So Nellie was surprised when Mary came up to her after school one day and said, "Do you sew, Miss Mooney?"

Nellie had looked into Mary's big green eyes and said, "Yes . . . a little." She didn't dare admit that she didn't sew much at all. If she did, all the farm women would be shocked.

"Would you sew me a dress, teacher? We have the material. We've had it since spring, but Ma's sick a lot and can't find time to do it."

"Well . . ." Nellie squirmed a little. The child was looking at her with large blue eyes. "Well, I guess I could try."

The next day, Mary had brought the print to school and Nellie had taken it back to the Hornsbergs. She was very thankful to Mrs. Hornsberg, who had a sewing machine and did most of the piecing. Nellie had done all the slow work, including holes for the pretty little pearl buttons she had bought out of her first month's pay. And now she could hardly wait to see the expression on Mary's face, for she bet the child had never had such a pretty dress before.

Nellie knocked, but there was no answer. She could hear the sound of a crying child so she cautiously opened the door and looked inside. Mary's two little sisters were pulling their two-year-old brother across the floor on his back — by the feet. When they saw Nellie, they dropped his feet and came running over to her.

"He won't go outside to play," the older one said. "Ma says to take him outside. She's sick and he won't leave her alone."

Just then Mary came through a doorway with the baby under her arm. Her brow was puckered into a deep worried furrow that alarmed Nellie.

"What's the matter?" Nellie asked.

"Ma's gone into labour. And I don't know why the doctor hasn't come. The pains are real bad." She gave a little gasp as though breathless herself. "Pa took the horse and buggy for the doctor over an hour ago."

Nellie knew that John Wheeler had had plenty of time to be back long before now and feared the worst.

Maybe he'd decided to stop off at the tavern in town. But surely he would have called the doctor first.

Mary put down the baby, who was dressed only in his flannel diaper and a light undershirt. He toddled unsteadily over to one of the other children.

A loud, half-stifled cry rose from beyond the kitchen. It seemed to be coming from a room on the right. Mary turned and ran back towards it.

"Wait," Nellie said. "I'll watch the children while you go for the doctor, but run, Mary!"

Nellie looked at the frightened children and said to the oldest, "Help me put on their coats and then you may play in the yard." She turned to the first child, but another loud cry came from the bedroom. "Your mother needs me, but I'll be checking on you. Stay inside the yard." The Wheeler farm had a large yard and a long lane — two hundred feet — to the main road.

Nellie went through the small door on the right and found herself in a hall. The sound must have come from upstairs on the far side of the house. She hurried up the stairs and then ran in the direction the cry had come from. Nellie rushed into the bedroom just as Mrs. Wheeler was starting to moan again. She stood there helplessly and wondered how women could tolerate so much pain in childbirth.

When the pain had passed, Mrs. Wheeler saw her standing there. "My dear," she said, "it's good to see you. I'm going to need help. I think my John must have stopped for a nip on his way . . ."

"Mary has already gone for the doctor. I'll watch the children for you, Mrs. Wheeler." The perspiring face before her relaxed a little. Nellie took a soiled handkerchief from the dresser and wiped Mrs. Wheeler's brow.

"Thank you, Miss Mooney. Now would you check on the young-uns? I'll be fine. I'm getting used to this."

Nellie wondered how she could ever get used to it. She turned into the hallway.

"Miss Mooney!"

"Yes," Nellie said as she stepped back inside the bedroom. "You better put on a kettle of water to boil. The doctor may need it. The pains came on so sudden-like this time that I wasn't able to do it."

Nellie turned quickly then and ran down the steps. When she reached the kitchen, she rushed to the woodstove. The fire was nearly out. She grabbed the poker hanging on the side of the stove and raked the low coals into a glow. The fire needed more wood, so she looked in the woodbox behind the stove. There were a couple of small sticks in the bottom of the box. She took them out and piled them on the low coals. Then she hurried out to the woodshed for more logs.

When she had the fire going, Nellie looked for the water pail and found it beside the back door. It was empty, so she took it out to the well halfway to the barn. She was thankful to see that the children had done as she said and were playing near the back door.

"Miss . . . Miss," the older girl called. "We're playing Daniel. You can be the king if you'll play with us."

"Later, maybe. Now, I have to get some water."

Nellie took the bucket that was sitting on the low stone wall around the well opening and let it down on the long chain. Then she started to bring the chain up.

Soon Nellie had the water heating in two large pans on the stove. By the time the doctor reached them, it would be ready. "But where was the doctor?" she thought. "He's had lots of time to get here."

Just then the door opened wide, and Mary, looking more distraught then ever, burst into the kitchen.

"What is it, Mary? Where's the doctor? Is he on another case?"

"I don't know, Miss. The doctor's wife said that he left with Pa. She said they left a long time ago. And, Miss, no one has seen them since."

Nellie stifled a gasp. She must not let Mary see her fright. Just then another loud cry echoed through the house. Nellie thought, "The baby must surely be coming and I can't help, I just can't!"

A short, distinct knock came to the door. Mary, who was nearest, opened it, and there stood Mrs. McClung in a brown cape that matched her usual brown hat. Nellie could have flung her arms around her neck and kissed her.

"Mrs. Wheeler is having a baby," she said. "Her time is very near, and we can't find the doctor or Mr. Wheeler."

A glimmer of disgust passed over Mrs. McClung's face, and then she said, "I see you have water heating. That's good. She took off her cape and draped it across the only empty chair. Then she quietly unbuttoned her cuffs, took them off, and rolled up her sleeves. "Is she upstairs?"

"Yes," Nellie said.

"I'll check on her. Keep that fire going."

"But shouldn't I go to find the doctor and Mr. Wheeler?"

Once again Mrs. McClung's mouth tightened in a fine line. She turned to Mary. "Now, dear, you run out and look after the children. Nellie and I will take care of your mother. Don't you worry."

Mary ran out at once. Then turning to a wide-eyed Nellie, Mrs. McClung said, "Don't look so alarmed, Nellie. This won't be the first baby I've had to deliver and it probably won't be the last. Try to find me some clean towels." Then Mrs. McClung hurried out of the room.

She quickly disappeared into the hallway, and as Nellie

started to hunt for the towels, she passed the table and noticed the brown-paper parcel containing Mary's new dress.

****

A week later, Nellie went over to see the new baby. She was carrying some clothes Mrs. Hornsberg had made. Although the trustee's wife spent a lot of time caring for her own home, she felt compassion for poverty-stricken families. She had made a nightgown and dress for each child and a number of diapers and shirts for the new baby. "Mrs. Wheeler's a proud woman," Mrs. Hornsberg had said, pressing the parcel into Nellie's arms. "She'll take them easier if you deliver them."

Mrs. Hornsberg had driven Nellie to the end of the long lane, and now Nellie was plodding up to the kitchen door. She dreaded this visit, for she didn't want to see Mr. Wheeler.

Everyone in the neigbourhood was talking about what had happened. He had arrived at the doctor's, and the two of them had started back to the Wheelers', but when they were passing the tavern, John had suddenly had a weak spell. He'd asked the doctor to attend to him and the doctor had taken a nip himself. Then they had started talking and kept on drinking. Both Mr. Wheeler and the doctor were dead drunk in the tavern while Mrs. McClung delivered the baby girl.

The whole community was buzzing with the news. They already knew about Mr. Wheeler but had thought better of the doctor. Now there was a rumour going around that a few influential farmers were hunting for another doctor to settle there. But doctors were hard to find so far from the big city of Winnipeg. So the community would likely have to forgive him. But John Wheeler was in another category.

Nellie walked to the door through the long grass. It had been trampled down only in the places were the chidren had played. They could almost play hide-and-seek in it, Nellie thought as she looked at the unkempt dooryard.

Mary opened the door and smiled widely at Nellie. She had obviously seen Nellie coming down the lane, for she was wearing the new dress. "It's beautiful," she said almost in a whisper. "And I'm going to take it right off. I just wanted you to see it first."

"I hope I will see it at school," Nellie said.

"Oh, yes. If Ma will let me wear it."

"How is your ma?"

"She's just fine. She won't be out of bed for a few days yet, but we're managing fine. And Pa's been home all week and helping."

Nellie noticed that the room did look much neater. The chairs were cleared of the children's clothes and the floor had been swept.

"Well, I have a few clothes for the little ones that I'd like to give your mother. May I see her?"

"She wants to see you, too. I'll just stay here where I can keep an eye on the others," Mary said.

Nellie went through the hallway and up the stairs to Mrs. Wheeler. She could not imagine what this poor woman must look like now after the hard time she had had.

To Nellie's surprise, Mrs. Wheeler was sitting up in bed nursing the new baby, looking better than Nellie had ever seen her. She smiled when Nellie came into the room, and her thin face and rested eyes looked almost pretty.

"Why, Nellie, I'm so pleased you've come. I've had

such an easy week of it in bed that I'm starting to get restless. But the doctor says I must stay right here for another few days. And I can't say I'm complaining much. My John's been waiting on me hand and foot."

"And well he might be!" thought Nellie but said, "I've brought you a few things from Mrs. Hornsberg — clothes for the children. Would you like to see them now?"

"Yes, you open the parcel."

Nellie folded over the shirts and diapers for the baby and then she held up each nightie and dress for the girls and the little play suits for the boys.

"Please, thank Mrs. Hornsberg for her kindness, Nellie," Mrs. Wheeler said, wiping away a few tears. "She's very kind, indeed. And I don't know how she did so much in a week."

"Well, she started after we made Mary's dress."

"It's beautiful, just beautiful. And she just loves it and wants to keep it in her drawer. But I said no, she should wear it to school while it still fits and let folks see how pretty she is."

Nellie nodded and sat down on the chair beside the bed. "I don't know what I would have done, Nellie," Mrs. Wheeler continued, "if you hadn't come when you did."

"Mrs. McClung would have arrived in time."

"No, I don't think so. She happened to be going into the drugstore in town when she saw Mary running down the street. I guess she put two and two together and decided to check on us. She wasn't far behind Mary." She took the baby from her breast and started to rub her back gently. "We're grateful to both of you ladies. So we plan to call our new little one Nellie Anne, after Nellie Mooney and Annie McClung."

Nellie opened her eyes with surprise and said, "The name does have a nice rhythm to it."

"Now there's something else I wanted to talk to you about," Mrs. Wheeler said as she put the baby back to her breast. "I want you to know that I'm not blaming my husband. I suppose everyone in this town is talking, but mind you, I'm not blaming him. You see he thought the baby would take longer coming . . . more like the others did, and he felt the need to have just one drink. He's such a sympathetic fellow and can't stand to see anyone in pain. He said he just had to brace himself a little to face things. So he and the doctor stopped to have just one, but they kind of forgot themselves and I guess they felt so lightheaded when they left town that they lost their way. Then when John did get home, it was too late. He just went to bed and slept and didn't know about the baby until the next day."

Nellie sat quietly with her hands in her lap, but she was filled with indignation at the way this woman was accepting such treatment from her husband and still standing up for him.

The silence hung heavy between them.

Mrs. Wheeler glanced over at Nellie. "I suppose you can't see why I ever married John. But you should have seen him in our courting days! He was the sort of man who would take any girl's eye. My! I wish you could have seen him then!"

Then a shadow crept across Mrs. Wheeler's face as she continued. "I suppose I shouldn't have married him, though. There was a fine man wanted me, and life would have been different with him, for he was steady and thrifty, but he was the most homely man I have ever seen, and I wanted something to look at!"

Nellie sat very still. She had heard those words before,

for she and Hannah used to play a game of listing the best attributes for a husband. Hannah had always put "moral worthiness" at the head of her list. And what a fight they had had over it.

Nellie remembered with a pang that she had always listed a fine face and carriage as qualification number one.

22

A loud tap sounded on the schoolhouse door, and everyone turned to look as a small boy about eight years old walked in. Nellie looked coolly at the raised heads as she passed down the aisle to the door, and all pupils turned back to the lessons before them.

It was 9:30 on a warm day for late October, and the boy stood by the open door in his rolled-up shirt sleeves. An old straw hat, the same colour as his hair, shaded his face, and he looked up at Nellie with wide, frightened eyes. They were clear blue and surrounded by long lashes almost too blond to see. His turned-up nose was covered with a splattering of light brown freckles. In his right hand, he clutched a black tin dinner pail.

"Hello," said Nellie, giving him her friendliest smile. "Won't you come in?"

"Yes, Miss," he said quietly, then burst out: "Pa said,

'Go on and give the damn thing a whirl,' so I'll stay for today." He looked nervously around the class as a low ripple of laughter spread through the room. Nellie frowned at her pupils but did not reprimand the boy.

When they reached her desk, Nellie asked him, "What is your name?"

"Robert John Ricker, Miss."

"My name is Miss Mooney. You will call me Miss Mooney from now on. Now, please take off your hat, Robert."

"My folks call me Robert John," he said as he removed his hat.

"Thank you, Robert John," Nellie said and gave him another big smile. This time, he seemed to relax a little. Nellie had heard Mrs. Hornsberg speak of the family. Five years ago, his father and two brothers had settled in the area with their families, along with Robert John's grandfather, an old man who ruled the clan. They lived among themselves and came to town only for necessities and without their families. They never went to a picnic, church, or any gathering. So Nellie knew it was a big step for Robert John to come to school. And she knew that one word of criticism today would send him home again, probably never to return.

Nellie went over to the storage cupboard and surveyed her supplies. Her eyes were drawn to what seemed to be a chart or poster all folded into a flat piece. She resisted the temptation to see what it was and reached past it to find a new scribbler and bright red pencil for her newest pupil. She handed them to him.

"Gee, thanks, Miss Moon," he said.

Again there was laughter from the class, which Nellie silenced with a stony stare; then she turned to Robert John. "Now we must choose a seat for you."

The trustees had added five more seats, and fortunately there were still two vacant ones. She placed Robert John with the young students but on the side next to the older ones. Though he had never been to school before and had to start in the primer class, she thought it best to seat him nearer the older ones, since his language would need some training. Meanwhile, his vocabulary would have less effect on the older students.

Once Robert John was seated comfortably and had started drawing in the scribbler, Nellie went back to the cupboard and took the folded poster out and laid it on her desk. It unfolded into a huge chart showing the bad effects of alcohol.

When Nellie looked up, Esther's hand was waving. "Yes?" Nellie said absently.

"I can explain about the chart if you like."

"Yes, please come up here and tell me."

Esther approached Nellie. "A couple of trustees bought this chart two years ago," Esther said in a low voice. "It was very expensive. It cost forty dollars. But it was prepared by doctors and shows all the harmful effects of alcohol."

"Has anyone used it?"

"No, that's why father's angry. All that money wasted and it's just been chucked away in that corner of the cupboard."

"Thank you," Nellie said. As Esther walked back to her desk, Nellie's thoughts were racing. So it had been gathering dust, had it? Well, she would use it! She had wanted an excuse to inform people about the harmful effects of alcohol ever since Mr. Wheeler and the doctor's escapade. And besides, the town was not blameless either. Didn't she always wake up on a Saturday night to hear the loud drunken revelings — almost a mile away?

As Nellie went through the day's lessons, she kept thinking about how she would use the chart to show the children the evils of alcohol so that not a pupil of hers would ever touch the stuff. The real problem was not the noise the men made at night. It was the way they mistreated their wives and children and neglected their work.

Finally, the day drew to a close. Nellie was thankful that Robert John had been quiet: she had not had to reprimand him on the first day of school.

At dismissal, the students all rushed for the door and were soon gone except for Esther, who was cleaning the blackboards, and Robert John, who shuffled slowly up to her desk with his head hanging down.

"What is it?" Nellie asked.

"You may do it, now," he said.

"Do what?" Nellie asked.

"Kiss me."

Nellie cleared her throat. "I can't kiss you, Robert John, because if I do then I'd have to kiss all my students at the end of each day. And you can see that it would be quite a chore."

Robert John looked up then with great relief spreading over his face. "Wait till I get home. Pa said I'd have to kiss you every day. That's what kept me scared. The old goat!" He turned around, then ran down the aisle and out the door.

Nellie kept a straight face until after he had gone; then she and Esther burst into laughter. Nellie wondered if she would ever see him again.

The next morning, Robert John was there early. Nellie smiled at him as she set up the chart from the cupboard. She had studied it for hours the evening before. Nellie explained to the class how some doctors had studied these things for years, and how harmful alcohol could be to the body. She did not go into the moral aspects. She just talked about the physical effects illustrated in the chart. And thus Nellie gave her first temperance lesson to her students.

When she had finished, she smiled confidently at the students and hoped to receive some positive reactions to her lesson. Instead only Robert John's hand was raised.

Nellie looked around the classroom. Not another hand came up except his, which was now starting to wave in an agitated semicircle.

Nellie finally said, "Yes, Robert John."

"Did you make those pictures?"

"No. They are made by doctors in big cities. They have studied these matters for many years."

"Well, then, I'll tell you what they are — they're all lies! My father says a drink of licker is better than a meal; he has been drinkin' since he was ten, and he was never sick in his life. So those doctors are lying, teacher."

Loud gasps of horror came from the older girls. The big boys soon wiped the smiles off their faces when Nellie's sharp eyes swept around the room and back to Robert John.

"Some people can do anything and still be healthy. I knew a little boy once who could run through the snow in his bare feet, and he never got sick. And a man in our community bragged that he had never had a bath, and he stayed healthy. But most folks can't behave like that. So one example, like your father, isn't enough to prove that alcohol is not harmful. Besides, your father is not old yet. Someday the drinking may hurt him, too."

****

Three weeks later Nellie found herself in her classroom on a Sunday afternoon. She was nervously setting up e temperance poster in front of some blackboard otes she had made. She had never intended to give is talk on the harmful effects of alcohol to the community, but here she was giving a command performance at the request of the school board.

The news of Robert John's comments had spread pidly through the community, and some thought at Nellie had been too lenient with him. Others greed with the boy. So the trustees decided that Nellie ould give the same talk to interested parents and ommunity members to show them what had caused e fuss. Nellie had a feeling that the trustees were just ying to make more use of the poster a clever salesman ad persuaded them to buy. This meeting would help justify the expense of it. But what if no one liked the resentation or the poster? Then the trustees would lame her.

Sunday afternoon was the only time that many of ese busy farm folk had to themselves. Wouldn't they refer to sleep? Nellie hoped so, for she was feeling orse by the moment. She didn't want to be in the iddle of a feud. These people and their children eemed to find enough to fight over without her adding to it.

After she finished setting up her poster, Nellie sat own and looked at the clock. It was ten to three, and e meeting was scheduled for three o'clock. She oked out the front window at the snow stretching out cross the prairie. The weather had taken a sudden urn since Robert John's arrival at school that balmy ay three weeks before. As Nellie was contemplating he beauty of the scene and daring to hope that no one ould show up, she noticed three sleighs coming along he road. Probably the Hornsbergs, she thought. But Ir. Hornsberg was unlikely to speak out at a public meeting. Nellie had discovered that his ravings at th train station the day she had met him were just a way letting off steam. And Mrs. Hornsberg would neve speak publicly without her husband's permission.

All the same, Nellie shivered a little and went back add a log to the stove at the centre of the room. Sh wouldn't need to add more. The meeting wouldn't b long; her part was only twenty minutes.

Right at three, in came the families of the pupi who were helping her with the display. There ha been lots of enthusiasm in class when she had tol them about the presentation and asked for help. S eight students had made their own posters and wer displaying them at the side of the room. They woul come up in turn and explain their drawings and the point out, on the main chart, the source of thei knowledge. Well, at least her students hadn't let he down. All eight had arrived. If she became speechles they would carry on for her.

Her relief did not last long, however, as more an more people poured into the little room. At 3:05, sh decided to start. The seats were all filled, and a crow of men stood at the back. It was so hot in the littl school that she wished she had not added the extr wood. One man at the back opened a window.

Nellie's heart was thumping as she stood up. What i she said something stupid? What if she didn't sa enough and everyone started to fight anyway? Sh could barely control the children's squabbles. How or earth could she keep the parents from fighting? And al because of her. She had given them something else tc divide them. Still she firmly believed in the informatior that she was presenting to them. So she would give it he best. She gulped back her fears and stood looking side ways at the chart as she began to explain the harmful effects of alcohol on the body. She read the doctor's quotes directly from the chart.

The audience was not hostile but not overly friendly either. So she turned to Esther, who came over with her presentation. Esther's parents and even her aunt and uncle from Manitou had come to see her. They all beamed with pride. The audience clapped loudly at the end of her three-minute talk. "Now, Tommy," Nellie announced.

He was a small boy who lisped badly, but he had insisted on helping, and his drawing was one of the best, so Nellie had agreed. He came forward and his freckled face lit up with a big grin. "I'll juth path thith around," he said. "It'th all there!" He proudly started his drawing of a diseased liver going around the room.

There were exclamations of awe. Whether they were because of Tommy's artwork or the disease, Nellie was not sure. But the effect was good, for everyone clapped when his work was finally passed back to the front. Beaming, he went to the back of the room to stand beside his smiling father.

The student presentations continued. Each performance was followed by loud applause and smiles on the faces of the parents. Time was dragging on and the presentation was well past the half-hour when it finished.

In a low voice, Nellie said, "Now there seems to have been some problems in the community about this lesson. In fact, the trustees tell me that they have received many complaints. Would you care to voice them now so that we can decide if this lesson should continue to be a part of the curriculum?" She stood white-faced and waited.

There was a lot of mumbling among little groups, but no one spoke out. Nellie waited what seemed like an eternity. Finally, Robert John's father stepped out from the back of the room. "Well, I ain't sayin' I'm through, because I don't know, but I do say, a fellow is a damn sight better without licker, and I think these pictures are . . . good stuff for kids to see."

That clinched the matter. Those present voted for Nellie to continue the lesson, and the trustees, too, were pleased.

Nellie was ecstatic at her victory. The demon rum had been defeated forever. She had delivered the community from this evil. In the future all the women and children would be safe and their husbands sober — except for Mrs. Wheeler. She would not be safe. Her husband had not come to the meeting. But there would be no more Saturday night sprees now that the real scientific facts were known.

Nellie carried this delusion with her for almost an entire week.

The following Saturday night, however, Nellie was rudely awakened by loud noises. She ran to the window to see what she thought she had heard. The sight was sickening.

In the soft starlight, she could see two teams of horses and wagons galloping wildly along the road back from Hazel. The drivers were obviously drunk and they were shouting and flailing their beasts with whips.

Nellie slumped back into bed and pulled the blanket over her head to drown out the sounds. Finally, she managed to fall asleep, only to dream that she was being chased around the school by a mad ox with blood running down its side.

23

"I'd love to ride in the caboose," Nellie said as she stood on the platform of the Somerset station in her new black coat with the Persian lamb collar, cap, and gauntlets. Mr. Hornsberg was persuading the conductor to take Nellie on the freight train that was leaving for Wawanesa in a few minutes. The biweekly passenger train had left Somerset the night before, but Nellie had been staging a concert then, and tomorrow was Christmas Day.

The conductor smiled at Nellie. "Sure, you can come along with us. We'll be pulling into Wawanesa early Christmas morning, so you'll be able to get in on all your family's festivities."

"Merry Christmas, Mr. Hornsberg," Nellie said. "It's been a good term."

"It has been that, Nellie, and we'll miss you around the place till you get back in January."

Nellie clutched her bag and a basket of sandwiches and baking that Mrs. Hornsberg had given her. Then she climbed up into the cupola of the caboose. Snuggling under a soft buffalo robe, she gazed out over the fields and thought back over the fall term. She had a happy feeling that it had ended well. The whole community had turned out for the Hazel School Christmas concert. They had clapped loudly and laughed even more loudly at the students' performances. It was a great feeling, Nellie thought, to see them laugh together like that. And now they had something else to talk about — not just their old differences.

She hadn't saved them all from alcohol, but she knew she had made some impact for good on their lives, and surely that counted.

Another highlight of the term had been her visits to the McClung family. She had often been invited to their home, and her respect for Mrs. McClung had grown each time. She treated her sons and daughter equally, and all did dishes and other housework. The women were not expected to wait on the men. It was a home of sharing.

In early November, Mrs. McClung had actually invited Nellie to a political meeting at Manitou. Nellie had looked forward to the event for a whole week. She felt she was definitely in the right place at the right time as she sat beside Mrs. McClung in the audience that night. Mrs. McClung, as usual, looked strong and composed in her neat brown coat and soft hat. But the evening had gone downhill from there. As the collection plate came around, Nellie and Mrs. McClung had put two signed questions on it for the speaker, the Honourable Thomas Greenway. They had asked him if he was in favour of extending the franchise and giving women homesteading rights.

Mrs. McClung had told Nellie how complacent some comfortably married women can be about the hardships and trials of less fortunate women — women with inadequate husbands and many children, widows with and without children, and especially single mothers. "The law does not protect these women," she had said as she turned to Nellie. "According to Canadian law, women are persons in matters of pains and penalties, but not in matters of rights and privileges."

Mrs. McClung had been quick to add that this law had been passed in 1876 in England and had not, as yet, been used here. "But there it stands and it certainly can't help women. It should be stricken from our laws." Nellie had heartily agreed.

Except for the speaker, no man there spoke to them the whole time they were there. And they were the only two women present. They had watched the speaker closely as he unfolded the papers that held their questions. He had read them quickly and then slipped them into his pocket without answering them. Only at the conclusion did he look over at them as he told the audience that women had a most important role in helping their menfolk to vote correctly. Then he had smiled at Nellie and Mrs. McClung, shaking his head the way a parent might shake his head at small naughty children. Nellie could feel Mrs. McClung stiffen in her seat and Nellie also felt indignation rise within her. What chance would women have in court or in getting the vote when such a law was on the books? She could hardly believe it!

But Nellie was not sure if she could do anything about the plight of women by being involved in politics. It all seemed so dry and useless.

As they drove to the manse from the meeting hall, Nellie told Mrs. McClung how she felt. "I don't think I want to be a reformer after all," she concluded. "I can do my share of the world's work some other way, can I not? I want a big friendly house, white and glistening, under great spreading trees with a huge fireplace in the hall that will send out a welcome to the world . . . and there will always be good talk and great fellowship there."

"That sounds wonderful, Nellie, but how would you take care of the disadvantaged women that way? Would they come to your white, gleaming house? Would they feel comfortable at your table? And what would *they* go home to?"

Nellie was struggling with this thought as they headed into the McClungs' driveway. The world was gleaming white that night, and Nellie's heart skipped a beat when she saw Wes drive up not far behind them.

Once they had all piled out of their cutters and put the horses away, he had listened for quite a while to the women's complaints about the fruitlessness of the meeting. He always seemed to have an even temper in the face of great frustrations. Nellie had seen him often at the McClungs' since she had bought the fountain pen, but he had never asked her out.

"Why don't we go and get a treat at the confectioner's to cheer you two up," Wes said, exchanging a glance with his mother.

Mrs. McClung was too tired to go, so that left Wes and Nellie on their own. They discussed everything about the week's events, the possibilities of gaining more rights for women, and the coming Christmas concert. Then Wes had driven her home to the Hornsbergs in his cutter. As she got down off the cutter step, he'd pressed her hand and smiled at her quietly instead of saying goodnight.

After that, Wes had taken Nellie out to skating parties

and Young People's at the Church every Friday evening. Nellie always liked spending time with Wes, for they had good discussions about all kinds of topics, and Wes listened gravely to Nellie and treated her like an equal. Nellie had shared with Wes all her hopes and dreams about helping farm women, and he thought it a wonderful goal. She enjoyed his company, in fact, the company of all the McClungs, but she didn't think of Wes as her boyfriend just because she was seeing him on a regular basis. He was a good friend, and she was much too young to think of anything more permanent. She had to get used to being a teacher first. And then she would help women.

Suddenly Nellie noticed that the windows in the little caboose were iced over, and she felt chilled. It was almost dark, and clouds seemed to be gathering in the northwest. Nellie decided to go downstairs to see if it was any warmer there. One man was shovelling coal into the little pot-bellied stove while another was spreading out bread and cheese on the table. The smell of fresh coffee perking filled the little car.

"Help yourself, young lady. We have plenty," the conductor said.

"I'd like that," Nellie said, "but just a minute, let me get something for you." Nellie came back down with the basket of sandwiches, cookies, and cake that Mrs. Hornsberg had packed for her.

"My landlady is a great cook," Nellie said, putting the basket on the table. The men smiled, sat down, and helped themselves. Nellie poured herself some coffee and took a place at one end of the table.

"It doesn't look good," the brakeman said. "The snow is starting to come down now. It'll drift badly across the tracks in the low spots, and we may be stuck for the night." He gave Nellie a worried look.

"No need for alarm," the conductor said. "We have plenty of food and fuel. You'll be safe and warm here, Miss, even if we have to wait for the snowplough from Brandon to come and dig us out."

Nellie smiled back. She wasn't worried. "The only problem," the conductor continued, "is that we may be stuck for a day. I've seen that blooming snowplough take twenty-four hours to get through. And that means we'll be spending Christmas here on the tracks!"

Nellie smiled again to reassure them. She wasn't going to feel too badly until the train stopped at least.

After they had all eaten, Nellie took one of the top bunks and pulled a heavy buffalo robe over herself. Of course, it was impossible to change out of her clothes, so she just kept them all on. The winds were roaring loudly now and their progress was slow but steady. She fell asleep almost at once, lulled by the rhythmical movement of the train.

Sometime in the night, the train came to a lurching stop that jolted Nellie awake. She snuggled down into the buffalo robe, wrapping its sides around her, then went back to sleep again. The train would probably be moving again the next time she wakened.

But when Nellie next woke up, the train was still stopped. The fire was going and the storm was over, but they were definitely stuck.

"I hope the men running the Brandon snowplough don't wait till after their dinner to bring her out!" the brakeman exclaimed.

"Oh, they won't do that, George," the conductor said. Then he looked at Nellie. "I've saved some bacon and eggs and coffee for you, Miss."

"Thank you very much. But what do you mean about dinner?"

"Christmas dinner, Miss! We've been stuck for hours and it's going on eleven o'clock Christmas Day!"

Nellie sat down at the little table and sighed. At least there was one good thing: breakfast had never tasted better. Then the brakeman handed her a little jar of wild strawberry preserves to put on her toast, and she smiled with delight.

"I know this patch by the tracks back home," he said, "and the missus put them up in jars for us."

When Nellie had finished, they sat around the table in silence for a few minutes. Then the conductor said, "So you're a teacher. You don't look any older than my Laura, and she's still going to school."

Nellie smiled back. "Yes, I like teaching now. It was terribly hard the first month, but it's better now."

"I guess you had some concert. Mr. Hornsberg says that's why you missed the passenger train."

"We had a great Christmas concert. It was a lot of work, but the students did a good job and their parents liked it. I was proud of them all." Nellie smiled again as she remembered the happy faces leaving the concert with something more to talk about than their feuds back in Ontario.

"I suppose you had a lot of Christmas carols."

"Oh, yes, we sang lots of them. The children and their parents love to sing the carols."

"Would you want to sing a piece for us, Miss?" said the conductor.

So that had started it. Nellie sang one carol after the next, and then she repeated recitations from the children's program piece by piece. Then they started to sing the carols together.

They were singing "Joy to the World" so loudly that they could hardly hear the voice of the ploughman shouting, "Anyone home?" outside the caboose.

It was mid-afternoon before they were ploughed out and now, as they pulled into the train station at Wawanesa, it was past seven o'clock. They had had to travel very slowly, and Christmas would be nearly over, Nellie realized. But she was happy, all the same, for she was going home.

From the cupola window, Nellie saw Jack waiting with buffalo robes over the horses. She hurried down the first floor of the caboose to get her things together. She had bought presents for all the family, and her bag was bulging.

When the train stopped, Nellie hurried out the door and down the steps. She jumped off the bottom step and set down her load. Then she wrapped both arms around Jack.

"Oh, Jack, I'm so glad to see you."

"I knew you'd persuade those railway men to take you on the freight. You could talk the ears off a corn-stalk." Jack smiled and picked up her bag and the empty food basket.

"It's too bad you were stuck in a freight train for Christmas."

"Oh, Jack, don't take it so hard. I'm fine and I'm home now. Is everyone there still?"

"Yes." Jack gave her that sad smile again. "They're still there and anxious to see the new schoolteacher in the family."

"Well, I'm not the first. How's Hannah taken to teaching in the Northfield school?"

"Fine, I think. You know Hannah. She wouldn't complain even if she didn't like it. And she's been a God-send to Mother these past few weeks."

Jack helped Nellie up into the sleigh and threw the buffalo robe over her lap. "It's getting colder now the storm has passed," he said. "It'll be a frigid night."

Jack flipped the reins lightly over the horses' backs, and they started speeding along the snowy trail, the bells jingling cheerily.

"It's *so* good to be going home," Nellie said. She looked up at Jack's handsome features and wondered if he had invited Abigail over. "Have you invited anyone else for Christmas, Jack . . . anyone special?" she asked. Surely Jack wasn't still moping over Abigail. She was away teaching somewhere and hadn't been able to make it home for Christmas.

"No, it's not that, Nellie. I haven't heard from Abigail since she left for her new school, but I'm not concerned. We were only good friends like you and Bob were."

"Yes, Bob. How is he doing?"

"Fine. We don't see much of him since he married last May, but we hear he's sure raising some fine Clydesdales. He had them at the Fall Fair."

"Well, what is worrying you, Jack? I can tell there's something wrong."

"It's father. He's been mighty sick with pneumonia. It's passed now, but he's not picking up the way he should."

"But he's never sick. I didn't know he had pneumonia."

"Mother didn't want to worry you, so we didn't write you about it. We figured he'd get much better by Christmas, but I guess it's better for you to know about it now than when you see him. He's failed badly these last few weeks."

"I can't think he won't be fine in a while," Nellie said. "We all know what a great nurse Mother is. She'll have him back to himself in no time."

"I hope you're right. We've asked the doctor to call in a specialist from Brandon. He'll be coming in a few days. Maybe he'll have some new medicine to help."

Jack flipped the horses' reins against their backs, and they sped along more quickly.

"Thanks, Jack, for coming to get me. It must have been a miserable day for you standing around here."

"I didn't stand around all day," Jack said and a little smile lightened his face.

"You went back home, then?"

"No."

"Well, where did you go?" Nellie was really curious now. "Did someone take pity on you waiting at the station and invite you in to share their roast turkey and plum pudding?"

"You could say that."

"Well, tell me."

"Well, I met a Mr. Wilkie, who came in to pick up freight from the train, and when we found out it was going to be late, he invited me back to his place at Treesbank for Christmas dinner. So I went . . . it being closer to Wawanesa."

"I'm glad. I hated to think of you waiting here all day."

"Well, Mr. Wilkie talked and talked. He's a fine man and we had a good visit. And the meal was something wonderful. Do you know there are seven daughters in that family? So we were waited on in style, I can tell you."

"Jack! You always have been waited on in style. But tell me about the daughters. Were there any your age?"

"Well, I didn't ask them to line up and tell me their ages, but they were good-looking. I think I'll go back."

"Well, tell me her name."

"Whose name?

"The one you're going to court."

"Wait a minute. I'm not planning to court anyone, just now. I've got enough on my hands, worrying about

Father. But someday, I may go back to see Barbara. I think she's a little too young to court just now and I'm not in any hurry, but maybe . . . "

"Tell me about her."

Jack was looking straight ahead with a dreamy look in his eyes. "Well, first of all . . . she's beautiful. She has large brown eyes and thick dark brown hair and a soft sweet voice."

Nellie saw Jack relax a little as he talked about her. Maybe Jack would court this girl and give up his plan of never marrying.

They rode along in silence for a while. In spite of her light chatter about the Wilkie sisters, a cold heaviness had settled over her and no amount of light talk could lift it. She could hardly wait to get home and see their father.

When they turned into the laneway, Jack drove more slowly and pulled up almost to the door. Nellie jumped down before they came to a stop and did not wait for her belongings. Jack would bring them all, including her gifts. She had been so pleased to have the money to buy a present for everyone but now it didn't seem important. The only thing that mattered was seeing her father.

In her hurry Nellie stumbled right into Nap, who jumped up on her and tried to lick her face. "Good boy," Nellie said and gave him a bear hug, then she ran to the kitchen door with the dog at her heels.

Nellie burst through the door into the lamplight. Will came rushing over. "Nellie, you're finally here!" Beside him was his wife, holding Fred, their toddler.

"Nellie, you're a sight for sore eyes," Mother said as she rushed over to pick up Nellie's new black coat. Nellie had just thrown it off, onto a chair. "Here, sit down by the heat. You look cold to me." She pulled a stiff-backed wooden chair over to the stove.

Nellie's face was flushed from cold and worry. She must see her father. "Where's father?" she gasped out, still standing.

"Right here, Sparrowshins," he said, as he came shuffling out from the downstairs bedroom. He was in his night clothes and was wrapped in a long plaid robe.

Mother hurried over, took his arm, and helped him into the rocking chair by the stove. Then she rushed into the bedroom and came back with a blanket for his lap. She tucked it around his legs. "Now, now, Lettie, stop this fussing," he said, but he smiled up at her all the same.

Nellie hurried over to him and gave him a big hug and kiss. His weather-beaten cheek felt rough against her soft lips. He surely was healthier than Jack thought. "You are getting better, aren't you, Father?" she said and drew the chair up next to him.

"Yes, yes. Now, don't look so alarmed. I'm well on my way. How could I not be with a such a fine nurse as your mother? A lucky man, I was, the day she said, 'I do,' and she's been doing for me ever since."

Nellie was surprised to see a tear trickling down her mother's cheek. An even colder feeling came over Nellie then. She could not remember when she had ever seen her mother cry.

"So what did you do while you waited for the snowplough all day?" asked Lizzie, who was now hugging a plump, gurgling baby boy, born just after Nellie had left for Hazel. Mother and baby were both rosy-cheeked and smiling.

"Oh, we sang, and then we . . ."

"Nellie Mooney! You don't mean to tell me that you joined in the singing with those men." Mother turned around and stared at Nellie. There was not a trace of a tear left. Mother seemed back to normal again, Nellie thought.

"Yes, Mother, I did," she said quietly.

"You talked to those men! You sat down with those men! You should have kept your distance up in the caboose."

"In fact, I recited. I acted out the whole Hazel School Christmas concert for them," Nellie said with reckless abandon, for she knew her father would approve. "I had to play all the parts, but it was no problem. I knew everything by heart from training the students."

"You will go too far, one of these days, my girl, and I fear for you," Mother said with a tone of doom in her voice that silenced Nellie.

"Oh, Lettie, Lettie, leave her be. She did the right thing celebrating our Lord's birth with these men." Father smiled his approval at Nellie.

Then Will spoke up. "There's no need to worry, Mother. I know the crew and they're fine men — all of them."

"Well, come now, Nellie, and have a bite," Mother said. Nellie walked over to the table and sat down on one of the chairs. She could not believe the plate full of mashed potatoes, turkey, and dressing. Then Hannah came with a pitcher full of golden, bubbling gravy and poured it over her meat and vegetables.

"How's Northfield school these days, Hannah?" Nellie asked.

"I like it all right," Hannah said, "but it's hard sometimes, trying to fill Mr. Schultz's shoes." Hannah had taken over for him when he'd moved to a school nearer his farm and family.

"Have you seen anything of that theology student

lately?" Nellie said as she reached for the butter and buns.

Hannah laughed, "No. Too bad, I guess. I think he got frozen out at Mrs. Ross's boarding house in Winnipeg." She giggled so loudly that Nellie could see she didn't feel too badly about losing him.

"What's this all about?" Father asked with a twinkle in his eye.

"You tell him, Nellie. You always have such a knack for telling a good story."

"Well, Father, Hannah had a great admirer when she was going to Normal School in Winnipeg. He used to come to call on Hannah every Sunday evening — after church, of course — and stay until ten o'clock. Well, Hannah's landlady let her boarders entertain their guests in her parlour. But it was never heated!"

"A cool welcome, I see," Father said.

"It was cool all right. Harry wore his fur-lined coat the whole evening, and I had to wear my heaviest coat, too. It wasn't very romantic."

"Yes, there's more romance at home these days, I hear," Nellie said. She knew Hannah had gone skating and dancing with Bert Ingram a few times already this winter.

"I don't know what you're talking about, Nellie L. Now you finish your pudding. We're going to sing a few carols."

Nellie held her tongue but gave Hannah an impish smile.

****

"You're a pretty old man, Mr. Mooney, and have lived your life. You can't expect to live much longer," the doctor said brusquely, shaking his head.

It was the second day of the new year, and Jack had driven to Brandon to get the specialist to check on Father's declining health. He had come in, nodded at Mother, warmed his hands by the stove, and asked to be taken to Father. After a short examination, he gave his gloomy assessment to Jack, Nellie, and Mother. "I don't know why Dr. Anderson called for this examination. Surely the man can recognize the end when he sees it." He put his instruments back in his bag and closed it.

"He won't last long. It's a general breakdown of the system. And after all, he's lived far longer than most folks."

"You have only discouraged him," Jack said sharply, looking the doctor straight in the eye.

"Well, I can't perform miracles," he said. "Grow up, boy."

Jack rose, and for a minute, Nellie feared for the doctor. Then Jack got hold of himself and sat down with a sigh. "We don't expect miracles," he said in a calm voice now, "but we did expect a little kindness."

"Oh, your father would want to know the truth. It gives him time to get his house in order."

"His house has been in order for many years," snapped Mother. "He made his peace with God many years ago, and he has not an enemy in the world. . . . We knew he was a very sick man, Doctor, and hoped you might be able to prolong his days. But thank you for coming anyway. Jack, hurry and hitch up the cutter."

Father slipped into a deep sleep after the doctor left, but the next morning, he woke up feeling much better. "That ould trap," he said in his rich Irish brogue, "would rather tell a man he was dying than anything else. . . I'd like to make a liar out of him . . .

and I believe if I could just get past March, I'd go another year. Anyway I've had a long life, and a pleasant one. I've lived near the soil and feel friendly to it. It will lie lightly on my bones."

Nellie noticed that Jack seemed to take new hope and comfort after their father's words and she, too, started to relax a little. After all, the doctors could be wrong. They weren't God.

That afternoon, the Reverend Mr. Howarth, the Methodist minister from Stockton, came and was welcomed by the family.

Mother, along with Jack and Hannah, gathered in the little bedroom while the minister read the fourteenth chapter of John's Gospel. "Let not your heart be troubled . . . I go to prepare a place for you."

After the reading, the minister prayed and they sang a hymn together. Once again, their father joined in singing the familiar words. Nellie and Jack exchanged hopeful glances as they watched his energy increase.

But the next day he did not wake up, and his breathing was very shallow. So Jack went for Will and Lizzie. Mother would not move from the chair by his bed, where she held his thin, chapped hand. When Nellie and Hannah urged her to go out to the kitchen for a bite to eat, she would say, "He might wake up and be too weak to call me. I want to be here for him."

They all took turns going in to watch with their mother. As his breathing became heavier and heavier, they knew that his lungs were filling with fluid. Finally, Mother called them all into the little bedroom.

They stood around their father's bed and watched. Will had his hands on the back of Mother's chair and looked protectively over her head to Father. Lizzie and Hannah stood on the far side of the bed, while Jack and Nellie stood at the foot. Nellie grasped the corner of the wooden bedstead.

When her father's deep rasping breath seemed to miss a beat, Nellie's own breath caught in her throat in a sharp little catching sob, and then she felt Jack's steadying hand on her shoulder.

It was then that they heard Nap start to howl just outside the window, and the loud mournful howls just kept coming. So in a few minutes, Jack stepped lightly to the door and across the kitchen to let the dog inside.

Nap followed Jack right into the bedroom and stood beside the bed with his fur bristling. Still as a statue, the dog stared at Father's white face.

Choking back the tears, Nellie watched as her Father's heavy breathing become fainter and fainter until she could no longer hear it at all, and when his face blanched white and was still as stone, Nellie knew he was gone.

24

A flood of memories swept over Nellie as she sat staring at the empty classroom. She could hardly believe that her first year of teaching had ended. Just five minutes before, the last pupil had passed through the door.

She flushed with pride at the cheery farewell her students had given her. It was the last time she would see them together as a class. The next year, she would be teaching in a four-room school at Manitou. She could hardly believe her luck at getting such a good job. Still she would miss the children from this community. She looked thoughtfully at all the fresh bouquets of flowers on her desk in their odd assortment of vases. Robert John had brought her wild roses packed in a thick china cup, and Mary Wheeler had given her a small bundle of violets held together by a sopping wet rag.

After everyone had left, Mary had come running back inside the door and up the aisle. She had flung herself in Nellie's arms and cried. Nellie had tried to reassure her that they would get a nice new teacher. But Mary would not be consoled until Nellie told her she would visit her at home in the coming year. After all, Manitou was not that far away. So Mary had wiped away her tears and left with a half-smile on her face.

Nellie knew that no matter how many schools and how many children she taught, she would always remember these children from her first school. She had learned as much from them, it seemed, as they had from her.

Esther and her brothers had gone on home ahead, each with an armload of her teaching supplies, for the few things Nellie had started out with had been supplemented with more books as she was able to afford them. On her desk still sat the set of Dickens's books that Will had given her for Christmas. Nellie started to pack them in a little cloth bag. Even the close print had not deterred her from reading the long, tea-coloured pages. In fact, she felt a kinship with Dickens and his writing.

How many times that winter, she had wept over the pages as she read. She could see how Dickens made people cry for the poor and underprivileged. If only she could do for folks what Dickens had done. Yet who could do what he had done? Who could champion the poor as he had? It would be hopeless to try to emulate so great a talent even if for the right reasons, she thought.

Still, Dickens had not had a great education, and yet he had achieved great things. So maybe she could, too. But could she stand the agony of trying and failing? Wouldn't it be better to marry and have a family and forget all about her great ambition to help farm women? Maybe she would fail. But she knew she must try even if she did fail.

A tear fell on the cover of Dickens's *Oliver Twist* as she thought of writing a book one day. She would write about hardworking farm women — from their point of view. And she would show the world that the poor are not often happy. Her books would deal with reality.

She could picture her story now. It would be about a poor but brave family, struggling against poverty. And the heroine would be so courageous . . .

"Nellie! What's the matter?" Wes McClung was standing in the doorway of the school looking at her with deep concern.

Nellie straightened up quickly. "Oh, nothing," she said somewhat sheepishly, wiping away a tear.

"Nothing?" he said, walking towards her.

"Well, I was thinking about the family I'm going to write about some day and how I'm going to help women."

"And you'll do it, too, Nellie. Never doubt that." Wes looked fondly at Nellie as she finished whisking the rest of her books into the bag.

Then Nellie smiled at Wes. She liked this tall, handsome fellow who believed in her. It would be nice to be in Manitou next year. She and Wes could see more of each other then. She took the bag of Dickens's books from her desk.

"Let me carry that," Wes said. "I've come to drive you home. Our best buggy and horse are waiting. And if I can persuade you, we'd like you to join us for supper tonight."

"I'd like that," Nellie said. "but Mrs. Hornsberg may have planned something already."

"I stopped on my way over to the school. She says that she'll be agreeable either way."

"I'll go then," Nellie said. Since she would be catching the train back to the farm tomorrow, she was delighted to be going to the McClungs' this evening. She would miss them all this summer, especially Wes. She hadn't told her family about him, for she didn't know how serious their friendship would become, and that way she wouldn't have to explain if he went out of her life as silently as he had entered it. Still, it would be a long summer without seeing him. She hoped he would write.

Wes drove the horses slowly along the dusty road, and his red hair shone in the bright afternoon sun. It was still early, for Nellie had let the children out an hour ahead of time — a tradition for the last day of school.

"Nellie, I have something I want to say to you, something I've been intending to say for some time, but I wasn't sure before . . . so I've left it until now." Wes sounded very serious.

Nellie felt a fear creeping over her. Surely, he was not going to propose. She was too young — just too young to be tied down. And so was Wes. He was eighteen and she was seventeen. Still, it was not unusual to see a couple tied down with a family already begun at that age.

Nellie did not want to marry Wes — at least not now. But she knew that she did not want to say goodbye to him either. Would he spoil their wonderful friendship by asking her to marry him?

She'd lost Bob as her friend after he had asked her to marry him. Now was she going to lose Wes in the same way? She couldn't say yes now. She had to have time to live by herself. She needed to plan her life more before she married — that is, if she ever did. Nellie did not raise her eyes from the back of the horse swaying along slowly in front of them. She drew in a little gasp of air and waited.

"I've just found out I've been accepted at the University of Toronto to study pharmacy," Wes said.

Nellie sat bolt upright with surprise. Then she stared at him and threw both arms around his neck. "Oh, Wes, that's wonderful. I'm so glad for you."

"I'm leaving next week to go to Toronto for the summer. I can find a better paying job there and get ready for the fall term."

Nellie could not believe this was all happening so fast. She was not feeling quite so elated now as she realized that she might not be seeing Wes for a very long time — maybe never.

"But I'll write, Nellie," Wes continued, "and I hope you'll answer my letters."

"Of course, I will," Nellie said quickly.

"Good! I've enjoyed our talks together. I'll miss you, Nellie, I will." Wes sounded sad now.

"Oh, I'll polish my writing skills on you, Wes McClung. You'll be getting so many letters you won't have time to miss me. And you'll be busy with your work, too. I hear the pharmacy course is almost as hard as medicine."

"Yes, but I'll enjoy it. And, Nellie, if I meet anybody else, I'll tell you. And I want you to do the same."

"Yes, I will, Wes. And in the meantime, we're best friends."

Epilogue

Nellie and Wes were married five years later, in 1896, and lived in Manitou, where Wes had his pharmacy. Nellie no longer had to worry about being a farmer's wife. They had four sons and one daughter. The first one, Jack, was born in 1897, and the last one, Mark, was born in 1911. Nellie's choice of mother-in-law did prove to be wise, for it was Mrs. McClung who encouraged her to find time for her writing. One day, not long after Paul, the third child, was born in 1901, she came to do Nellie's housework, insisting that Nellie use the time to write a short story for a contest run by *Colliers'* magazine. By the end of the day, Nellie had written the first draft of the short story, "Sowing Seeds in Danny," which eventually became the first chapter of a novel by the same name. Nellie won no prize for it in the contest, but an editor from Wm. Briggs Publishing House in Toronto saw it and liked it. In 1908, *Sowing*

Seeds in Danny was finally released. It became a bestseller in Canada and did well in the United States, too, where it was published by Doubleday, Page & Company. Nellie received $25,000 from the sales of this book, a very large sum of money in those days, and it opened doors for her as a speaker.

Nellie had not forgotten the problems caused by drinking or the difficulties faced by women on the farms. She realized that the two problems were sometimes linked, since many women suffered because their husbands or boyfriends drank. So she joined the Women's Christian Temperance Union, an organization that fought against the sale of liquor. Before long, she began to fight for women to have the right to vote in elections.

In 1907, Nellie made her first speech — at a conference for the Women's Temperance Union in Manitou. There she saw hope come into the tired eyes of overworked farm women, and she knew she would have to carry her message to other women.

Nellie was a witty speaker and was soon in great demand. She travelled around the country, giving readings from her books and speaking out for women and their rights. Although she had a busy schedule, she took great care to make sure her five children were well looked after at all times. In those days a woman who did not stay at home to take care of her children could easily be criticized for child neglect. Once, her youngest son, Mark, got very dirty while playing outside. One of the older boys rushed him home by the back lane, saying, "Quick now! It's a good thing I got you before the *Telegram* got a picture of you — Nellie McClung's neglected child!"

In 1911, the McClungs moved to Winnipeg, where Nellie learned of the harsh conditions in which women worked in the factories. She and Mrs. Nash, another fighter for women's rights, persuaded the Manitoba premier, Sir Rodmond Roblin, to visit one of the offending companies with them. The premier was shocked by the filth and gasped, "For God's sake, let me out of here. I'm choking! I never knew such hell holes existed." The women had made their point, but in the car afterwards, their hope for improvements was dashed when he added, "I still can't see why two nice women like you should ferret out such utterly disgusting things."

Nellie would not stand for this and replied, "By nice women, you probably mean selfish women who have no more thought for the underpaid, overworked women than a pussycat in a sunny window has for the starving kitten on the street. Now in that sense I am not a nice woman, for I do care. I care about those factory women, working in ill-smelling holes, and we intend to do something about it, and when I say 'we,' I'm talking about a great many women, from whom you will hear more as the days go on." When Nellie assured Sir Rodmond that she would be back, he asked her if that was a threat. "No," Nellie answered. "It's a prophecy."

Though Roblin did stay in power after the next election, still a 1915 scandal in connection with the building of the new legislature in Winnipeg caused him and his party to resign, and the following election was a landslide for the Liberals. After suffrage workers obtained far more than the designated number of signatures for their cause, they persuaded the government that people wanted women to have the vote. One petition contained 39,584 names, and another, 4,250 names. A 94-year-old rural Manitoba woman had collected all the names for the second petition. On January 29, 1916, a bill to give women in Manitoba the vote was unanimously passed by the Legislature. Manitoba was the first province in Canada to give women the vote. Between 1916 and 1940, the other provinces followed. The House of Commons granted this right to Canadian women in 1919.

In 1914, the McClungs moved to Edmonton, where Nellie was elected as a Liberal member of the Alberta Legislature in 1921. Nellie was not the first woman to sit in the Alberta Legislative Assembly. (Mrs. Louise McKinney, elected in 1917, had preceded her, as the first member of *any* Legislative Assembly in the British Empire.) In 1921, Nellie also gained popularity as a speaker at the Methodist Ecumenical Conference in Britain, where she was the only woman delegate from Canada.

Back in the Alberta legislature, Nellie continued to fight against the sale of liquor, a position that naturally made her unpopular with the Alberta Hotelkeepers' Association. During the election of 1926, they warned her that they would do anything they could to cause her to lose her seat if she did not stop attacking liquor sales. Of course, Nellie did not stop fighting, and she did lose her seat.

Nellie is perhaps best remembered for the fact that she was one of the five women who fought to have women defined as "persons" under the law. Because women did not have the rights and privileges of persons, they were prone to many injustices. When a woman married, for example, her property automatically became her husband's to do with as he pleased. (The husband, however, kept full rights to his own property.) Emily Murphy, magistrate for the province of Alberta, and Nellie McClung and three other women sent a petition to the Supreme Court of Canada about this matter. But the Supreme Court confirmed on April

24, 1928, that women were not persons. (Imagine what little chance a woman would have in any court case against a man when the court and judge based their decisions on this assumption!) Not to be stopped, the five women launched an appeal in the Supreme Court of England. They could not afford the expense of this undertaking themselves, but they persuaded Prime Minister William Lyon Mackenzie King to send the petition along with other business items at the expense of the Canadian government. As a result, on October 18, 1929, the Privy Council of England declared that women were persons.

In 1935, the McClungs moved to British Columbia, where Nellie became the first woman to sit on the CBC's board of governors, and in 1938, she became a delegate to the League of Nations. She died in 1951 at the age of seventy-seven, and her husband died seven years later.

Nellie Mooney McClung, who did not learn to read until she was ten and who grew up being told to "hush her talk" in the presence of adults, became a famous speaker, novelist, and activist. This is how the *Toronto Star* described her: "Nellie McClung, prairie reformer, suffragette, parliamentarian, author, newspaperwoman, and Canada's leading pioneer feminist, kept right on fighting for women's rights with the cheery battle cry: 'Never retract, never explain, never apologize — get the thing done and let them howl.'"

Notes

Most of the incidents in *Nellie L.* are true but dramatized and enhanced with fictional detail to bring them to life. *Nellie L.* follows Nellie L. McClung's autobiography, *Clearing in the West,* very closely, with some exceptions.

Nellie did not run in and win the race with boys at the picnic, but as indicated on page 106 of her autobiography, she did want to. She complained about her long, cumbersome skirt and wished for matching drawers (culottes, today) so that she could run more freely. Nellie had another brother, George, two years younger than Will. And instead of having just one friend, Bob Ingram, she had two — I have combined characteristics of both to create a fictitious one. Occasionally, I insert fictional names to give life to minor characters.

The following quotes, unless otherwise noted, were taken from *Clearing in the West.* Occasionally, I changed a quote slightly to make it more readable for today's students. Significant changes in Nellie's language are indicated in what follows as a paraphrase. The numbers along the left refer to the page numbers in *Nellie L.*

4 "Don't I wish . . . it's hard.": Mrs. Mooney 107.
4 "forty people busy": Mr. Mooney 27.
5 "She was everybody's friend.": 9.
12 "There will be no whiskey drinking . . . just bad times." : Mrs. Mooney 107.
17 "The rocky Jack Thomas . . . cared to be richer.": Nellie 10.

29 "it was melting . . . between her fingers.": Nellie 108.

31 "It did my heart good . . . pies that will melt in their mouths.": Mrs. Mooney 110.

33 "her feathers fluffed out and her temper ruffled.": 86.

33 The next spring . . . her brood everyday. (paraphrase): 87.

34 "a bit stern, but the greatest . . . to keep their hearts from breaking.": Mr. Mooney 36.

34 You know, when Christ . . . "and yet serious too and earnest.": (paraphrase and quote): Mr. Mooney 37.

34–35 "*Shule, shule, . . . avoureen, schlana.*": Mr. Mooney

40 "The ripening grain made golden squares and bands on the prairie, and blue haze shrouded the horizon.": 115.

43 "Sure and it is a grand country . . . and a bed to lie on.": Mr. Mooney 130.

43 "She never cost me a doctor's bill.": Farmer Brown in Nellie L. McClung, *Jane Brown,* p. 1.

44 "out loaves of bread": Farmer Brown in Ibid., p.1.

44 "Ignorance holds families together.": Johnny Lance 63.

45 "Take it aisy, lad.": Mr. Mooney 131.

51 "a big girl . . . won't learn anything": Mrs. Mooney 92.

62 "The snow . . . deep and white.": Nellie 146.

62 "We call horses brutes . . . makes him forget that someone is depending on him.": Mrs. Mooney 163.

64 "Every fence post . . . glistening white.": 146.

64 The runners . . . into Nellie's face. (paraphrase): 174.

68–69 "My little girl is dying . . . the best child I ever had." (quote and paraphrase): Mrs. Mooney 79.

82–83 "The heights of great men . . . of the mind.": Nellie 137–38.

86 Nellie sat half-crouched . . . and his life would be over. (paraphrase): Nellie 141.

90 "For without are dogs,": Rev. Hall 134 and Revelation 2:15: *The Holy Bible: King James Version.*

90–91 " . . . and sorcerers . . . and maketh a lie.": Rev. Hall 134–35. and Revelation 2:15: *The Holy Bible: King James Version.*

94 "Even when I wrap it in [George's] fur coat, it freezes.": Mrs. Burnett 165.

95 "It is not Louis Riel . . . be restored.": Hannah 169.

100 "A soft answer turneth away wrath": Mr. Mooney 179.

100 "Strange, isn't it Mr. Mooney, that . . . Governments still think a bullet is the best argument.": Mr. Schultz 179.

101 It will come . . . those two principles. (paraphrase): 179.

101 It was the "nutmeg" and "lilacs after rain" and "wild roses pressed in the pages of an old . . . book": 180.

103 "Remember this country . . . feeling themselves superior.": Mr. Schultz 186–87.

105 "Indian ponies hitched to carts and strange dogs.": 187.

105 "The smell of . . . filled the air.": 188.

111 "Strike into this one . . . all watching you.": Mr. Mooney 203.

113 . . . started in on the "Fisher's Hornpipe" . . .

with her hands on her hips.: (quote and paraphrase) 205.

127 "Do not fear. . . . Tell it to Jesus alone.": The Salvation Army band 232.

127–28 As the band played . . . had done her best. (paraphrase): 232.

130 "a voice for the voiceless": Nellie 281.

133 "Maybe it will be a good thing . . . to have the conceit taken out of you.": Mrs. Mooney 237.

133 "No, perhaps not, but you talk too much . . . smooth you down.": Mrs. Mooney 237.

135 "Having passed . . . at Winnipeg.": 238.

137 "Say, kid . . . did you fail?": Jack 241.

137 "Don't take it so hard . . . in some ways,": Jack 241–42.

138 "I'm sorry . . . picking on me.": Nellie 242.

144–45 "Now, Nellie . . . come home and be welcome.": Mrs. Mooney 258.

146 "Demand decent salaries . . . and wear clean linen.": Mr. Goggin, the principal of Winnipeg Normal School 251.

148 Well, take a good look . . . so you better eat up. (paraphrase): Mr. Hornsberg 263.

157 "She's the only woman I've ever seen that I'd like to have for a mother-in-law.": Nellie 269.

168 "he is a voice for the voiceless . . . a flaming fire": Nellie 281.

190 "mind you, I'm not blaming him.": Mrs. Wheeler 285.

190 "I shouldn't have married him . . . I wanted something to look at!": Mrs. Wheeler 284.

191 "Hannah [had always] put 'moral worthiness' . . . a fine face and carriage as qualification number one.": Nellie 285.

193 "Go on . . . the damthing a whirl.": Mr. Ricke
289.

195 If I kiss . . . quite a chore. (paraphrase): Nelli
290.

195 "Wait till I get home. . . . scared, the old . . ."
Robert John Ricker 290.

196 "Well, then I'll tell . . . never sick in his life."
Robert John 291.

196 I knew a little boy . . . may hurt him too
(quote and paraphrase): Nellie 291.

200 "Well, I ain't sayin' . . . for kids to see.": Mr
Ricker 292.

200 "But there would be . . . were known.": 292.

203–04 "I don't think I want . . . and great fellowshi
there.": Nellie 310.

214 "You're a pretty old man . . . to live much
longer.": the doctor 330.

215 "You have only discouraged him . . . in the
eye.": Jack 330.

215 We don't expect miracles . . . a little kindness.
(paraphrase): 330.

215 "His house has been order . . . to prolong his
days.": Mrs. Mooney 330.

215–16 "That ould trap . . . It will lie lightly on my
bones.": Mr. Mooney 331.

227 "Nellie McClung, prairie reformer, suffragette . . . and let them howl.'" The *Toronto Star*
in *Clearing in the West,* back cover.